Holding the torch down, he saw the face of a man in the uniform of a Roman centurion. Hissing between his teeth, he called Attila to him. He pointed to the face with the swollen tongue lying in a pool of dried vomit.

"This," he whispered to Attila, "is the man from the walls of Orleans, the one who led the attack on our rear at the fields of Catalonia. I remember him because of the scar on his face. See how it runs from his eye to the corner of his mouth." Ch'ing chided himself for being foolish and even considering the remote possibility that this was the foreigner who had served the Emperor Tzin over a hundred years ago. That man was obviously and most certainly dead.

Attila poked the body with his sword, pricking the cheek. There was no doubt about it, the Roman was dead. "What killed him?"

Ch'ing moved away from Casca to examine several other bodies. He hissed and backed away, covering his face with his hand. "Plague," he hissed. "They have all died of the plague."

CASCA:

THE DAMNED

#7

**BARRY
SADLER**

ACE CHARTER BOOKS, NEW YORK

An Ace Charter Original

Published by arrangement with the author.

ISBN: 0-441-13580-3

First Ace Charter Printing: October 1982
Published simultaneously in Canada

Manufactured in the United States of America

Ace Books, 200 Madison Avenue, New York, New York 10016

PROLOGUE

Casca listened to the slapping of the waves against the hull of the ship, the flapping of the single sail in the shallow breeze, which was taking him away from the past—on to what? He stayed in the shade as much as possible to keep the sun off his still tender skin and placed himself where he could catch some of the breeze pushing them forward. He was so damned tired; nothing had changed for him. Nothing he tried ever made any difference. The future was the same as the past; only the names changed. He grimaced when an edge of a plank dug into his ribs. To ease the pressure, he sat back, hands wrapped around his knees, looking across the easy rolling waves to Syria where he had boarded ship at Antioch; beyond, behind the mountains and deserts, lay Persia: the empire of the Sassanid Kings and personal domain of Shapur II, King of Kings.

Persia! The name brought a bitter taste to his mouth. The sleeve of his burnoose fell back when he moved his hand to push away a droning fly. Red welts exposed themselves to the sun. He pulled the sleeve back down. Under the flowing robes his entire body was much the same—a mass of seared burned tissue. A gift from Shapur to repay him for his loyalty and service.

He still found it difficult to sit near an open fire without wanting to scream. The smell of roasting meat made his stomach turn, for it had not been long ago that he had smelled his own roasting flesh. Of all the pain he had ever known nothing was as bad as those minutes on the stake where the fires ate at his body. Flames washing his flesh, sizzling, cracking the skin open to expose raw red meat to their searing touch. He shivered uncontrollably, his skin rippling in remembrance.

What was it Samuel the merchant had said to him the first day he set foot inside the walls of Nev-Shapur? That Persia was not for the likes of him. He had snorted bitterly, then; for where was there a place for such as he? Never had he found anywhere he could call home for more than a few years. Always time drove him out to somewhere else he didn't belong. It had taken nearly a month from the time he had left the cave near Koramshar till he saw the distant wavering outlines of the first Roman outpost through the shimmering waves of ground heat. Calinicium. Cresting a rise he had stopped before going down.

Two names came to him as he'd looked back on the plains and valleys behind him: that of the man who had given him both glory and pain, Shapur II, King of Kings, Shaha shan ut Aneran. The glory of Ahura-Mazda whose symbol was the ever-burning purity of the sun. When a petitioner would approach his master, he would do so on his knees, hands covering his eyes, crying out, "Lord, I am blinded by your radiance!" For to all in Persia, Shapur was the sun by whose will fields would grow or cities die. Shapur was the instrument and personification of their god.

Casca's reward for years of loyal service—fighting

the wars of Persia to secure the frontiers threatened by savage tribes—was to be proclaimed a heretic by the Vizier Rasheed and put to the stake to have his body burned to ashes. That Shapur had believed Rasheed still pissed him off. But then the favor of kings is a fickle thing at best, and if they wanted to burn someone at the stake, it didn't require much reason to do so.

The other name was that of Imhept the Egyptian, who had taken him from the burning stake before his body was completely consumed. Imhept had nursed him back to health in the cave by the sea, then provided him with the money he needed to get free of the lands of Persia. If he were found alive in Shapur's domains it would mean a return trip to the stakes. Imhept had only been able to free him by claiming a debt owed him by the King that had been made in public. He had forced Shapur to live up to his word when he had promised to grant Imhept anything within his power. Imhept had chosen Casca.

The fly returned to buzz around his nose and though the little pest didn't touch his skin, the buzzing of the wings millimeters from the hairs in his nostrils made him feel like sneezing. He brushed the mindless creature away with the back of his right hand.

He didn't think that Shapur would have let the Egyptian claim him if he hadn't believed him to be already dead. He wished the little man of the Nile well.

He turned from his reflections to face the dim walls of Calinicium. It would be dark before he reached them. That meant he would spend one more night sleeping in the open. He longed for a warm bath and oils to ease the aches of his body and sooth the innumerable sore spots where the leather of his sandals or even the rough threads in the inner seams of his tunic irritated sensitive skin. He walked down the path leading to the gates taking his time. He nearly laughed at the thought of taking his time—for what did time mean to a man who was damned? Time only meant that he would go on to face more disappointments, more pain and always more killing: years and tens of years into the unforeseeable future where he would never be given the peace of death.

He sat by the gates along with about a dozen others who were waiting for dawn when the gates would open. He kept apart, staying to himself with knees pulled up to his chest and his robe wrapped tightly about him to keep out the chill of the night. He didn't sleep that night; there were too many thoughts pulling at him to give him any rest.

Casca looked to the west, where a dim line of gray was beginning to show. The rest of those waiting went about their morning ablutions finding quiet spots to ease their bladders and bowels. Those that had women with them had built small fires fed by camel and horse chips and were warming food. His stomach gurgled reminding him that he hadn't eaten since the previous day. From his pack a small bundle of dates and olives served as breakfast.

He could hear the changing of the guard on the town walls. Familiar orders that he had obeyed more than once. It gave him a feeling of comfort to hear the language of Rome, his native land, again after so many years away. From the great wall of China to the frontiers of Persia. How many leagues had he ridden and marched fighting one battle after another—and for what?

He fell in line behind a Syrian farmer pulling a reluctant donkey loaded down with grain sacks larger than the animal was. The sun appeared over the ridge he had crossed the previous day, sending single red beams of light sliding across the plains to strike the brick walls of Calinicium at the same time the gates were unbarred and swung open.

When he entered the walls the guards gave him a cursory once-over. One of them pulled his hood back to get a closer look at the face in the shadows. He wished he hadn't! The exposed face had red welts covering the right side and the skull was devoid of hair except for a few stubborn patches that were beginning to grow through the red welts.

Even with his amazing powers of healing, it would be some time yet before he had a face that wouldn't turn goat's milk into cheese. But he knew the scars would eventually be sloughed off like a snake's skin as the new tissue under them pushed up to the surface. The sentries could see the burns continue down from his neck to his chest under the loose robes. One of the guards started to take the pack containing his sword from him but changed his mind when the gray-blue eyes staring out from a skull face locked on his. He had no desire to inspect Casca further.

Calinicium was much the same as any of its counterparts in Persia. The only difference was that the tongue of the Roman Empire was heard more frequently and the uniforms of the military were different. For the rest it would be impossible to tell it apart from any other sunbaked group of flat-roofed, white-stuccoed buildings set in the middle of nowhere. It didn't take him long to determine there wasn't anything for him here and it was too near the borders of Persia. If he stayed he knew he would be caught up in the next war which was coming as certain as sunrise.

He was in Calinicium only long enough to trade a few of his small silver coins, stamped with the likeness of Shapur, for a donkey to help carry him the rest of the way to Antioch, two hundred miles farther west.

The rest of the trip to the sea had taken thirteen days; he'd been in no rush. During this time most of his scars, except for the deepest ones, had sloughed off leaving only tender skin that rapidly toughened. His strength was returning too. When he was alone with no one in sight he would remove the sword from his pack and exercise, working to get the muscles loose and limber, restoring flexibility to his wrists and legs. If anyone had seen him in those predawn hours dancing and parrying, thrusting at nothing, they would have thought him a madman and gathered their neighbors for a community stoning.

Antioch, the gateway to the Mediterranean, was an ancient city. It had been ruled by Medes and Persians, Greeks and Romans, and always it had prospered under whichever master it served. It was one of the most beautiful of cities with wide thoroughfares and parks lined with statues of the great men of Rome, where once stood statues of Alexander the Great or the infamous gods of the Phoenicians. He had no eyes for the riches of the city or the temples of marble that once served Venus and Mars where now the priests of the Christus held their rites. Selling his donkey at a price which brought him only a small loss, he followed the scent of the sea leaving the city to enter the port where ships from all over the world came to buy, sell and trade their goods: slave girls from Circassia, amber from beyond the Elbe, silver bars of Dacia and weapons from the foundries of Greece.

Ports have an aura to them that is uniquely their own, the mingled odors of spices and sweat, salt air and tar. He found what he was looking for tied up to a stone wharf packed with hides from Libya.

The weeks on the trader had completed most of his

healing process. There was even a new growth of hair covering what had been charred tissue. He was feeling nearly as fit as before and was ready to leave ship.

Now the door to Italy was before him. One more day at sea and they would reach Pisae to the north of Rome. He wasn't ready to enter the capital yet. He had been gone for such a long time that he wanted to find his way back slowly. To walk first in the clear fields of Italia, to sit and listen to the peasants sing as they came back from their fields and orchards.

It was with the feeling of a long-lost son returning that he set foot on the piers that served the Roman garrison of Pisae. He was home at last. North of Pisae was where he had been born. That had been when Julius Caesar had been master of Rome. It was too far distant to think about. He would for now try to leave the past behind him. Before him were the mountains and valleys of his homeland. That's where he would go.

CHAPTER ONE

He took his time walking the back roads through the hills, not looking for any place in particular, simply enjoying the feelings of a man who had returned home after many years. The only thing that didn't seem to change very much was the land. Men come and go, as do their religions and philosophies. Empires rise only to be forgotten, but the land remains; at least, Casca was thinking, it stayed the same longer.

He spent a week going from one village to the next. They were nearly all alike, whitewashed buildings, faded red-tiled roofs set on the sides of rocky hills where the labor of five hundred years had cleared terraces for their orchards and vineyards.

He had noticed a dourness to the spirit of the hill people. There was a spark missing in them; some villages were worse than others. In these, the presence of priests of the new religion were more visible.

Casca thought perhaps it was because the old ways die hardest among the peasants that they were more reluctant to give up their old gods. Several times when he stopped for water at farmhouses set away from the villages, he saw the small offering bowls for the household spirits, the Lares and Penates. If the mistress of the house saw him looking at them, there would be a flicker of fear in her eyes that passed when he would casually place a small piece of bread or cheese in the bowls.

He missed the sounds of music that formerly had been ever-present in the hills. It appeared that voices lifted for anything other than praise of the new church were frowned upon. Therefore, it was with surprise when one evening, at the hour of Venus, he heard the trilling of flutes and voices singing. Following the sound to a grove of olive trees set in a small glade, he laid down his pack, then snuck up to where he could make out the singers. The sight did his heart good. Maidens with wreaths of spring flowers in their hair danced in a circle around a stone carving so old that the features on it were no more than shadows.

A sheep had been sacrificed and an old man was reading the entrails for his village, telling the future of the coming seasons for them. Wine was flowing freely to the singing of paeans that were banned in Rome. It was the spring rite of Pan and Bacchus the villagers were celebrating. Not an orgy, but a time of welcoming the awakening earth, preparing her for the planting of new life.

There were certainly, though, a few figures to be seen in the shadows away from the circle that were doing a lot of heavy breathing. Casca walked into the circle. For a minute, the music and voices stopped as the stranger in their presence approached the altar of Pan. He stopped, filled a cup with wine from an open jar, then poured a libation to the spirits of the old ones and drank. The music and laughter returned.

The laughter was infectious and soon Casca was roaring with the best of them, dancing in the circle, an olive wreath around his brow, the words of the ancient songs coming back to his tongue without conscious bidding.

He found himself away from the circle, his head turning with wine fumes, a hot sweet mouth on his. One of the village girls had decided to sacrifice a bit of herself to a stranger.

He was just raising himself from her when his eyes saw a pair of boots in front of him. Then the lights went out, as a knob-ended club swung down. Casca's head pounded from both the wine and the lump the size of a goose egg on his head. Chains rubbed sore spots on his wrists and neck as the metal links tried to work their way to the bone. Behind him, similarly chained together in a coffle, were the rest of the offending villagers. They had been arrested for violating the Edicts of Theodosius.

Things had changed more in the Empire than he would ever have dreamed possible. He knew of the triumph of those calling themselves Christians; he had seen that the followers of Jesus were everywhere and their priests were powerful men. But he had never heard of the Edicts of Theodosius, which Honorius sometimes enforced with a passion. The law was being read to him and the others as they were being chained up:

> It is our will and pleasure that none of our subjects, neither magistrates nor private citizens, however exalted or humble may be their rank and condition, shall in any city or in any place, worship an inanimate idol by the sacrifice of a guiltless victim. The act of sacrifice and the practice of divination by the entrails of the victim are declared a crime of high treason against the state, which can be expiated only by the death of the guilty.

Casca shook his shaggy head; the world had turned around. Before it had been death to be a Christian; now it was death not to be one. He wondered what Jesus would have thought of the change.

He had seen Christians die in the arena for their "crimes"; now it appeared it was the turn of those the Christians called "pagan" to do the same for the identical reasons.

They were herded onto a trail leading to the road that they would take to Milan. They were kept under the watchful eye of a decurion with two squads of legionnaires to bring in the heretics. Once on the main road, they were joined by several hundred others who were guilty of the same offense.

It was afternoon before they entered the gates of Milan to face the hurled abuse of the masses. Garbage as well as invective were heaped on them, along with taunts of "Pagan!" and "Idolaters!"

Casca had seen that look on the mob's faces before; it was a combination of hate and pious superiority. Without ceremony, they were hustled through the streets to the galleries of the arena. It was not as large as those of Rome, or even some he had seen in Africa or Asia, but it was ample enough to seat most of the adult population which would fill the stands in the next few days.

He had heard that gladiatorial combats had been forbidden, but then it was the prerogative of power to be able to change laws as they wished.

Already in the pens were about a hundred other so-called pagans; separated from them, in chains, were others considered more dangerous than the heretic villagers—Goths and members of several Germanic tribes captured on the frontiers and brought in for this occasion.

It would please the masses to watch pagan Romans

12

and barbarians destroy each other. That over half of the Goths were Christians of the Arian sect made no difference. They were all heretics in the eyes of the Mother Church.

Casca knew one thing, the pagans would take up the sword more readily then would the Christians, who in the days of Imperial Nero had almost to a man refused to kill. They died in the belief that their death on the sands would make them martyrs and, as such, they would be guaranteed a place in their heaven.

Casca wondered who had the most courage—one who would die without raising a hand for his gods or the others. He settled down in a corner of the cell after kicking a couple of others out of the way to make room. He had been separated from the villagers by the decurion who, once he saw the scars on him, knew he was a fighter and put him in the cells with the Germans and Goths.

The stench of fouled straw covering the stones of the cells did nothing to make him feel any better; his stomach was growling and he had a hangover. He tried to make himself as comfortable as possible and get some sleep before the games opened on the following morning.

He knew it would be vastly different from the last time he had fought in the arena. These peasants had no experience with weapons. They would simply hack clumsily at each other until they made a lucky blow or their opponent dropped from exhaustion. If they were lucky, they would be matched up against one of the barbarians who would more than likely put a quick end to their anguish.

Casca thought back on his days in the arena. It had been brutal, true, but at least there had been a sense of professionalism among the combatants. The training style at the schools, where they entered at tyros and left as professional gladiators, at least gave them options—either to die on the sands, find freedom with the gift of the wooden sword, or even a chance to acquire great wealth by betting on themselves.

One of the Germans in the cage next to him spoke to him through the bars. His voice was rough, almost a choking whisper, as if he hadn't had water for a long time. Then Casca saw the reason. There was a fresh scar on the Barbarian's throat where the edge of a blade had almost opened the windpipe. The warrior was still fit-looking, wearing the homespun red trousers of his tribe and a leather vest. The gray streaks in his fair hair said that here was one who had survived much and lived longer than most of his people.

"Roman, are you ready to die in the morning?" A smile followed his throaty question.

Casca merely nodded his head. "I've been ready a lot longer than you will ever be, Suevii," he answered the barbarian in his own tongue.

The German was surprised. It was rare for a Latin to know any speech but his own.

"You speak our tongue well, Roman. Have you spent time beyond the Rhine or Danube?"

Casca nodded. "A long time."

"As a slave?"

"No, my furry-faced friend, as a warrior."

The German whistled between his teeth, the front two of which were missing. He took a closer look at the object of his attention, the scarred face, thick wrist cords, and muscled neck. "Then you must be a good fighter, for the northlands have no love for the sons of Caesar."

Casca grunted. "You'll find out tomorrow, so why talk about it? There is little likelihood that any of us will ever be set free since they forbid the wooden sword.

What difference would it make if you won or lost?"

The German hesitated a moment. Then, making up his mind, he said, "Listen to me. There may yet be a chance for us to make our way out of here. It has been said that the Emperor often takes men from the arena into his personal guard if they fight well enough. He has many enemies in Rome and doesn't trust anyone. He feels safer with men who owe their lives to him. Tomorrow we might have a chance if we can attract his attention."

Casca perked up. "What's your plan?"

"We become swordmates against all comers. Let the weaklings finish each other off. We lay back until only the best are left; then we make our move and challenge the lot of them. There won't be more than four or five of them. We will have little trouble between us. I think we will have a good chance of winning. Like most cowards, Honorius is impressed with bravery; he thinks he can buy it. Let's give him a show! What say you, Roman?"

Casca thought it over a moment. Hell, he hadn't had any better offers lately. "Agreed. But only if you swear by all the gods of the Aesir and on your father's name that you'll be true until this thing is done."

The German smiled. "You have spent much time in the black forests. Be it so sworn, on my father's name and the gods of the Aesir, that I will hold my faith with you. This I swear, as my name is Vergix of the Suevii, a councilor and war chieftain of the tribes. But you, Roman, what do you swear by?"

Casca laughed bitterly. "I swear by one-eyed Odin All Father, by Loki, Jupiter, Zeus, Ahura-Mazda, and a dozen others you have never heard of. I swear by them all."

Vergix frowned. "It is not good to take the will of the

gods lightly, Roman, but I accept your word. From this time, we are swordmates against all comers, even those of our own tribes." The two shook hands in the Roman manner to settle their agreement, wrist to wrist, and each lay back to get what sleep he could.

Casca slept as usual, his rest troubled by dreams. Rarely could he sleep a night through without the ghosts of his past coming to disturb his rest. He awoke before the first light, eyes sticky and sore. Rolling over on his straw covering he looked straight at Vergix. "What time's chow?"

Vergix indicated with his head and Casca saw that several slaves were entering the confines of the holding pens carrying steaming pots. One of the slaves passed out wooden bowls as those behind ladled out their only meal. A thick mixture of boiled barley and pig slopped into Casca's bowl. It was not appetizing, but it would fill the gut and they knew they would need the strength later in the day. As Casca shoveled the food into his mouth with his fingers, he heard a distant rumbling. For a moment, he thought it was Vergix's stomach growling; then it came again, louder, a deep-throated coughing that could only come from the lungs of a lion. Vergix noticed his attention. "There will be beasts in the arena today. How many or what kind, I don't know."

Casca called over one of the serving slaves. "What time do the games start?"

The slave, a Dalmation, shook his head. "Don't be in a rush. You and the others won't go on until after the heat of day settles. You should be pleased; you're going to be the main attraction!"

Casca threw his bowl at the slave. "Smart-ass goat-herder! I hope you lose every tooth in your head but one and have an ache in it for the rest of your life!"

Vergix chuckled at Casca's curse. "You have a mean

streak, Roman, but if you didn't notice, the man is already toothless!''

Before noon, armed guards came in and began separating the men into groups; those who were old or disabled were put into one group and taken away. Shortly afterwards, they heard the sounds of the crowd roaring in pleasure and cries of dying men as they were fed to the beasts.

Those who were fit enough to fight were taken one at a time into an anteroom where they were outfitted in armor left over from the days when gladiators were treated like prized animals. Casca took the familiar helmet of the Galli with its fish-crested crown and perforated steel facemask.

Expertly, he checked over his equipment, exchanging one set of steel-mesh wrapping for his sword arm for another. Quickly, he tied the straps on properly, swinging his arm to see if it limited his motion. Satisfied after a couple of minor adjustments, he then selected a set of Thracian-style brass greaves to protect his legs and a wide leather-embossed belt that buckled in the back. His weapons would be given to him later.

The guards noticed his expert familiarity with the gladiatorial armor and made notes to lay bets on his winning against whomever he fought. Vergix also saw his new ally's familiarity and was pleased that his judgment of the man had been accurate. For himself, he chose that which he was most familiar with, and which would also make him stand out in the crowd when he and Casca made their play—a massive horned helmet with a brass strip running from the crest down to protect the nose.

As they were getting outfitted, the cries of dying animals reached them from the arena. The *beasterii* had been sent in to finish off the lions and leopards. It would be time now for the audience to take a break and get lunch from the vendors outside the arena, and talk over the morning's show.

The Emperor hadn't shown up for the morning games, but would be there to open the proceedings after lunch. This gave the arena attendants time to clean up a bit and spread fresh sand after hauling off, on long hooks, the remains of man and beast.

Many Christians refused to attend these slaughters, but even more did come and found great satisfaction in watching the heathens destroy themselves. Fresh in their minds still rang the screams of their own brethren. Revenge lies solid within the breasts of most men, and no amount of erudite philosophy and sanctimonious moralizing can cover it up completely. They found enough reasons for their attending—some to witness the final destruction of the heathen, others for the sheer pleasure of it, which they hid behind pious mottoes and phrases.

From the arms rooms, those next to fight were escorted to the cages next to the gates that opened onto the sands. Casca felt a familiar quickening of the pulse; the smell of blood was still on the warm air. Staying to himself, he began to exercise to loosen up muscles stiff from his night's sleep on the floor. Vergix merely sat in the shade and wished for a horn of ale before going out.

A fanfare of trumpets announced the arrival of the Emperor. Honorius, escorted by a squad of his praetorians, nodded pleasantly to the acclamations of the crowd.

Honorius, son of Theodosius, whose edicts against paganism he was enforcing in order to provide this day's entertainment, was a troubled man. He had none of the strength of the Caesars in his blood. His body was weak and soft. He had never fought in battle or faced any danger other than that of the court. His eyes were lackluster under the pressures of his office. Soft hands trembled as they gripped each other. The wreath of his forehead accented his thinning hair.

His role was not one he relished, but once he had power, there was no way for him to be able to give it up and live. Even if he abdicated, he knew that his successor would have him killed to prevent him ever being able to challenge him in the future.

The Visigoths, Vandals and a dozen other savage tribes on his borders, gave him ulcers. He didn't know what to do about them. But perhaps they would stay in Greece where Arcadius had granted them sanctuary. He wished that Stilicho would leave him alone with his constant warnings that the Goths were going to come against him soon. He needed this day's spectacle to reinforce his subjects' confidence in him and their savior, Jesus.

Today, he did have few barbarians to display along with those he had proscribed for their idolatry. Of course, he made sure the first Goths to enter the arena wouldn't be able to fight too well against his chosen favorites.

He had ordered the Goths to have one bone of their forearms broken, so that they could still carry their weapons. He knew the warlike spirit of the barbarians—they would have gone into battle with nothing but their teeth. He sighed deeply. If only Rome still had a small portion of that spirit. Instead, he constantly received complaints that the armor was too heavy and marches too long. The only soldiers worth a damn were from the provinces.

But enough of that! This day, he was still Emperor of

the city of the Caesars and secure behind the shields of his praetorians, most of whom were barbarians from tribes hostile to the Goths, or condemned criminals he had saved from death. He knew they owed their lives to him, and he had made it quite clear that when he died his will would make certain that they died also. They and their families lived only while he did. Honorius was not particularly bright, but he did understand fear and self-survival.

He was escorted to his box, decorated with royal purple and crucifixes set under a bronze Roman eagle. From his box, he addressed himself to the gamesmaster and, without further ceremony, gave the signal for the games to continue. He was uncomfortable with public speaking and tried his best to avoid it whenever possible.

The prisoners in the holding cages were given their choice of weapons as they were admitted to the arena. Vergix chose a battle axe, single-bladed with a wooden haft and spiked end. Casca took a long blade, similar in heft and feel to the *gladius iberius* he was most familiar with.

Before the fighters were admitted to the arena, they were told to line up, march out and to try to at least look as if they knew what they were doing. Legionnaires lined the way to the arena with drawn weapons and more legionnaires stood by in case the prisoners showed any signs of rebellion. Several of the would-be fighters were in such terror that they had to be prodded into the arena with red-hot irons. But all showed, not in the neat military line of the professional, but rather as frightened stragglers, or as bewildered but hostile barbarians.

Casca motioned for Vergix to follow his lead and

keep in step with him. The two led the way onto the hot sands, ignoring the other contestants. Vergix kept close to Casca, following his every move. With sunlight flashing off their bared weapons and armor, the two marched straight across the arena to where Imperial Caesar sat with his retinue. The two stopped about twenty feet away from the royal box. Vergix kept his eye on the Roman and followed when Casca raised his blade in salute.

"Ave Caesar. Te moritu salutus."

It was the almost forgotten salute of the gladiators to the Emperor: "Hail, Caesar. We who are about to die salute you!"

Honorius was surprised and more than a little pleased at this ancient act of honor to his royal person. These two would bear watching.

They were all herded back into their pens to wait their time to fight, with the exception of the twenty Goths who had had their arms broken. They were formed into a rough line, dressed in their native costumes—iron helmets, hide shields and scraps of armor. They looked fierce enough, but they would be no match for the elite troop of Roman legionnaires who marched in smart order toward a symbolic victory.

Casca had to admit that the legionnaires did look pretty good; they must be from the household guards. They were in full armor, carrying pilums, the Roman spear, and short swords sheathed on their rights sides. There were an equal number of Romans and Goths. The legionnaires, under the command of a centurion, were resplendent in silver-embossed armor and plumed helmets. They faced their bewildered and crippled opponents who huddled together like wounded animals. This was the opening act, and Honorius always wanted the first show to be good.

The legionnaires held their pilums ready, with shields to the front. When they had advanced to about thirty paces, they halted. The Goths began to see what was going to happen and started to spread out, holding their axes and long swords to the front. Before they could scatter, the centurion gave the command to throw, and the legionnaires hurled their spears, drew their swords, and advanced, while the pilums were still in flight. Five of the Goths went down under the barrage. The heavy-weighted points of the pilums penetrated the hide shields with ease. Even so, the Goths rallied and tried their best to take as many of the hated Romans with them as they could. Even with broken arms, they managed to drag down six legionnaires and finish them off before falling themselves.

The mock battle lasted little more than a few minutes and the Romans, naturally, were victorious. The crowd loved it, and threw garlands of flowers into the arena to honor their heroes.

Honorius was a little pissed-off that, even wounded, the Goths had managed to kill so many of his men. But anyway, the crowd was pleased, and he made the gesture of tossing a bag of silver to the commanding centurion to be divided among the men. The centurion saluted with his bloody sword, and proudly led his men from the field of slaughter.

Casca spat in disgust. As they went by, he called to the centurion: "Like to try me and my friend? Our arms aren't broken!"

The centurion flushed and tried to act as if he hadn't heard the jibe as they continued marching from the arena.

The time had come! The pagans were to be next on the agenda. They were admitted to the ring without even the customary drink of posca to cleanse their mouths. Casca and Vergix moved out fast to the far side of the arena, where they stood side by side, waiting and conserving their energy. Casca noticed that the statues to the gods were gone from their customary places around the arena.

The barbarians, by unspoken agreement, banded together in a group, eleven of them. Wolf-like, they started the fight by going after their frightened Latin opponents, few of whom had ever held a sword in their hands before. They went down under the blades and axes of the barbarians like sheep, calling for mercy and raising their hands in supplication, only to be jeered for their cowardice. The crowd pointed out to each other the difference between the courage of the Christian legion and the cowardly Roman pagans. They didn't seem to notice that the Goths were pagans too but were by no means cowardly, nor were the Germans of the Allemanni, Suevii and Marcomanni tribes, who hunted and killed Romans like so many sheep.

Twice, Latins tried to take shelter behind the scarfaced man and his fierce-looking companion, but Casca and Vergix drove them off, sending them back into the battle. Of the eleven barbarians, three died from lucky blows struck blindly in panic, four others suffered minor incapacitating wounds that would slow them down a bit. While the others were liquidating each other, Casca and Vergix stood apart, oblivious to the jeers of the crowd. The only reaction from the crowd in their favor was when ring attendants came out with hot irons to urge them to fight and were chased back to the safety of the holding pens. At this, the crowd realized that the two were waiting for something better.

When the barbarians had finished off the sheep, they at last turned their attention to the Roman and the traitor. The crowd grew silent; they knew they were about to see real fighting.

Honorius leaned over. His vacuous eyes lit with real

interest for the first time. Casca and Vergix moved their backs near the wall to prevent their opponents from getting behind them. The tribesmen formed a half circle. In a rush, they charged, only to find they were getting in each other's way. Three fell in that first rush; two to Vergix's axe, which split one's head open to the neck. He laid another's belly open, leaving him to crawl across the arena to die, trailing a ribbon of bloody intestines, jaws snapping at the sand.

The five barbarians backed off. The crowd began cheering, making wagers on how many the two against the wall would kill before they fell.

Casca spoke through clenched teeth to Vergix: "Now is the time to put the pressure on. They should be getting tired. From the look of them, they have been on short rations for some time. Keep moving and stay close to me."

Casca held his round shield low to the front. He lunged forward, striking first with the shield then with the sword. Vergix by his side, the two beat the barbarians back, cutting down one who had been slowed up by earlier wounds.

The two remaining tribesmen rallied enough to create a breathing space. The crowd fell silent again.

The surviving Germanics were hard-looking men who had reconciled themselves to their fates. One of them, a Vandal, came forward, a curve-bladed sica and round buckler held before him. He had a heavily muscled chest and arms. A single long braid of blondish-gray hair hung from under his iron helmet to reach to his shoulders. The other, a red-haired warrior from the tribe of the Marcomanni, came with him carrying an axe the same as Vergix's.

There was a feeling of expectancy in the stands as the men on the sands sized each other up, waiting. . . .

The Vandal threw back his head and screamed—

"Wotan!"—then hurled himself at Casca. The Marcomanni followed. It was sword against sword, axe against axe, as the four closed together in a struggle that could have only one ending. They fought without anger, just cold determination to kill before they died.

The Vandal drove Casca back, hacking a gouge out of his shield. His strength was great but it was the last of his reserves and he knew it. He rushed again, forcing Casca to his knees by nearly slicing off his face.

But a man who is not afraid to die, or who already considers himself dead, is doubly dangerous, especially when he knows his craft.

The Vandal lunged in with a straight thrust that Casca barely managed to block with his shield. The Vandal's sword stuck in it point first. Casca unexpectedly let loose of his shield. The weight of it forced the vandal's blade down before he could free it. That was all the time he needed. One straight lunge and his sword entered half its length into the hard striated muscles of the Vandal's stomach. As he fell to his knees, his weight pulled the blade out.

Holding his gut closed with his hands, he looked to Casca. "Well fought and well met, Roman." The mob was silent, in suspense, as if it were a thousand-headed creature.

The Vandal choked on a bloody bubble and smiled. "Give me peace, Roman." He leaned his head forward, exposing his neck. Casca understood. He would stop the pain for him. He struck with great force, hitting accurately at the junction of the vertebrae. The Vandal's head rolled free.

The last of the barbarians fought well, too, until a blow from Vergix's axe sunk into his chest to stop the beating of the warrior's wild heart. The stands went mad, silver coins rained down, women wept in passion, barely able to control themselves. Behind the mask of pious Christianity, the old Roman love of blood was still there.

The crowd began to chant in unison for the Rudis to be given. . . .

Honorius raised himself from his royal seat and stood at the edge of his box under the Imperial Eagles. He elevated his bejeweled hand, signaling for silence, and the crowd obeyed instantly.

Honorius was remarkable for nothing other than being extremely ordinary in appearance and manner. But, he was the Emperor. Lowering his hand, he pointed his finger at the warriors on the sands below him.

"It is the wish of the people that you be shown mercy. I am not adverse to granting you mercy, but there are two conditions. First, you must renounce all your pagan gods, and second, you must prove your valor against better fighters than those ill-trained savages there. Defeat two of my praetorians and you shall take their places."

The Emperor turned to the two nearest guards, massively built men, resplendent in the gilded armor of the Imperial Guard; both were extremely proud men from the same tribe of the Quadii. He pointed at Casca and his swordmate, softly ordering the guards, "Kill me those two men!"

The guards saluted and headed for the entrance to the arena. This was not the first time they'd been ordered to fight for their emperor. Honorius felt that it was good for his men to do a little bloodletting of their own now and then; it also served as a warning to his enemies.

As the two entered the arena, Casca noted that they were not armed with the *gladius iberius*, the regulation blade of the Empire, but instead they both carried the long swords of their homelands.

Casca wiped his sword hand across his loincloth to dry some of the sweat and blood which was making his grip slip a bit. He nudged Vergix, whispering, "This could be our chance. You take the big one and keep close to me, but watch out where you swing that damned meat cleaver—you nearly knocked my brains out twice."

Instead of waiting for the two praetorians to come to them, Casca and Vergix moved out across the sands, Vergix swinging his axe slowly back and forth. He stooped and picked up a shield made of ox hide, grinning at Casca.

The attendants, who had been waiting to draw away the last of the bodies, stayed in place. The crowd tensed, anticipating the action. It was well known by all that when the Emperor sent in his personal guards, it was to be a good show.

The praetorians moved confidently, almost with disdain, toward their adversaries. They were men used to being the victors. They'd killed many times; this would be nothing new to them. But this time, they were unaware that they were facing a man who'd trained at the school of Corvu the Lanista. The men they'd killed before were warriors from savage tribes, or legionnaires who'd been convicted of a capital offense. They'd never fought a professional who had won the wooden sword from the hands of Imperial Nero.

The fact that their two opponents had just killed several barbarians did not impress them much. They'd done the same thing themselves more than once. Besides, they were fresh now, and these two criminals should be about worn out.

Casca concentrated on his breathing, sucking air in

through his nose, keeping his mouth closed. He tried to muster enough saliva to spit, but failed. The heat was building under his helmet, sweat ran freely down his face. If not for the strip of cloth tied around his forehead, he would have been blinded by his own salty fluids. As it was, enough of his body's moisture still collected in his eyebrows and sent intermittent beads of sweat down to sting his eyes.

The praetorians stopped their advance at the approach of Casca and Vergix. They looked questioningly at each other. They were used to inspiring fear, not having their victims come to them. Ignorant savages, they evidently did not know whom they were facing.

The guards both carried round shields with lightning bolts radiating from the center boss. Casca went into a crouch, still using two blades. Vergix moved around to the side of his man, drawing him away from his comrade.

Casca moved, the two swords weaving and striking, trying to search out an opening in the other's guard. It didn't take him long to realize that he had an easy kill on his hands with this one, if he wanted it. The Quadii was big and strong but not very talented.

Casca toyed with him, waiting until Vergix finished his man, or was killed. Vergix was about evenly matched to his foe, and they beat at each other like two great bulls, head-on with no finesse. Vergix put an end to it by gathering all of his strength and smashing down with his axe, straight into the praetorian's shield. The blade of his axe sank into the shield almost half of its depth, nearly severing the man's left wrist where he was holding onto the inner shield straps. At the same time, Vergix pulled forward. There was nothing the praetorian could do. He had been taken unaware and was now off-balance, being jerked forward. As he moved, Vergix moved quickly to the guard's rear and jerked off the helmet. Forming a fist, he struck the praetorian violently at the base of the neck. The sound of the man's neck breaking was clearly heard and the crowd loved it. He started then to go to the aid of Casca, but was waved back by the Roman's hand. He wanted no help. They were here to put on a show. Vergix had done his part, now stage center belonged to Casca.

The surviving guard began now to know fear. Casca parried and lunged, the tips of his swords reaching in and knicking the other in a dozen places until his entire face was covered in a mask of free-flowing blood.

Casca could sense that the crowd was getting impatient for the kill now. He drove in, forcing the other back, and locked his sword against the hilt of the praetorian's. Dropping the blade in his left hand, he grasped the man's shield. Angling his body around, he twisted the praetorian to his knees, released the shield and wrenched the sword from the man's hand. Casca grabbed him by the armor, where it joined at the neck, and jerked the guard to his feet. He dropped quickly to his knee and pulled the man over his shoulders, bearing the entire weight of the other. Grunting with the strain of the lift, he rose to his full height, standing erect, the big man helpless now on his shoulders. He started moving, swinging from side to side, picking up speed with each half-turn. When he'd reached sufficient momentum, he released his hand at the man's thigh, retaining the grip at the neck with the other, allowing the man's own weight, combined with the motion, to force him down headfirst directly to the ground. The impact crushed the other's skull in its own helmet.

There was pandemonium in the stands and it took several

minutes before even the Emperor could quiet them enough for him to be heard.

Honorius was well pleased; his face flushed, he rose amid the excitement. His voice reached out over the arena: "You have been victorious and now there are vacancies that must be filled in the ranks of my personal guards. If you will now renounce all heathen gods and practices from this day forth, and allow yourselves to be baptized in the name of the living Christ, I will accept you into my guards. If you refuse, then the fate you receive will be of your own making. How say you?"

Casca spoke for both himself and Vergix. "We thank the people and you, Caesar. From this day we renounce the ways of the old gods and accept the Christus."

The audience went into a fervor of joy mixed with blood lust and religious zeal. Two lambs had been brought into the fold of Jesus.

They left the arena under a rain of flowers and the pleased eye of Honorius. Casca felt a mixture of contempt and pity for the Romans and their pathetic Caesar. But the important thing was that they were free again.

Two guards from the praetorians came for them, taking them first to the baths to cleanse them from the day's butchery. Vergix had bathed under protest, but Casca had noticed that the hot steam of the baths had brought an involuntary sigh of pleasure from the barbarian, even though he'd claimed that bathing was unhealthy.

After the bath, they were escorted to the commander of the guards, a tribune, for orientation. Before he would issue them their uniforms and equipment, a priest would see to their baptism. The priest took them to the river close by and they were forced to suffer the indignity, as far as Vergix was concerned, of being submerged three times to wash away all their earthly sins, to be born again as Christians. The only effect

Casca felt from the second bath of the day, other than a slight chill, was bitterness at being forced into accepting the religion and worship of the man he'd slain.

After the dunking, they were taken to the armory and issued the gilded armor of the praetorian guards, including the red-plumed helmet, and their weapon, a fancy sword with silver pommels. Vergix admired himself in a polished copper mirror, thumping Casca on the back and bellowing, "By one-eyed Loki, this is certainly a fine set of goods we've been given."

Casca warned him to watch his tongue in referring to his old gods. It was well known and demonstrated that these Christians had damned little tolerance, as he should well know by now.

The association with Vergix was good for him, though he never felt as close to him as he had to the giant Glam Tyrsbjorn of Helsfjord. Vergix still helped to ease a lot of Casca's troubles with his basic philosophy: It-don't-make-no-difference-what-happens-the-world's-still-full-of-bullshit was too logical to be argued with.

The cavalry contingent they were assigned to was sent more frequently on reconnaissance patrols. Each time they went out they returned with the message that the Goths were nearer and closing on Rome. Casca knew that in his heart Vergix was hoping for the success of Alaric. He didn't blame his hoarse friend; if their places had been reversed he would have felt the same. Vergix, for his part, would probably have deserted the first day he was set free if it hadn't been that Casca would have been held responsible for him and punished.

In spite of the racial differences, he liked the smaller, scarfaced Roman even if he was a bit weird. He took it upon himself to try and bring the Roman back into the real world—or at least to his thinking the only one that mattered—which was the world of plenty of soft women, good beer and an occasional fight to keep your spark up.

Over half the praetorians were from tribes outside the borders of Rome. Vergix fit right in with them but had a little trouble adapting to the discipline of taking orders from anyone that outranked him. He obeyed commands only reluctantly and was frequently reminded that if he became too big a pain in the ass there could be arranged a return trip to the arena or perhaps to the headsman's axe. However ten days of having to guard the imperial persons of Honorius and his sister Placidia brought him into line.

Casca told him to keep his mouth shut and just play the game. After all it could be a lot worse and the duty shifts they pulled were not very demanding. There was plenty of free time for them since the guard mounts rotated so that they were on duty only four days in six. Vergix appreciated this, for it gave him time to investigate the better whorehouses that Ravenna had to offer. Vergix cared for nothing; as long as his belly was full and there were coins to tinkle in his purse, he was content enough.

When they were on guard in the palace, Casca saw that messengers came and went with increasing frequency and each time they left, Honorius looked more worried. His soft cheeks would pale at each new piece of information about the movements of Alaric. At night he had a full squad of armed praetorians stand guard at his chamber doors, always within earshot, with orders to kill anyone that approached without proper orders.

Vergix had a knack for gathering gossip and soon knew more about what was transpiring behind the closed doors of the Emperor's councils than most of Honorius's ministers did. The hoarse Nordic had taken up with a Bithynian slave girl with big ears and even larger tits. From her he found out most of what was said in the inner chambers and relayed it to Casca.

When he asked Vergix how she knew so much, he was reminded that slaves are rarely considered people with any intelligence and their masters tend to talk too freely around them. To them they are no more than another piece of furniture that can move and do their bidding.

Honorius adamantly refused to return to Rome even when he received word that the city was certain to come under attack. He would not leave the safety of the mountains and the walls that surrounded Ravenna. Rome would have to take care of itself. He was not about to expose himself to the embarrassment of being captured by savages or even to suffer personal pain. It was much better, he thought, to save the empire the indignity of having the imperial person placed in jeopardy by remaining where he could give hope to all of his desperate people. As the father of his country he was not expendable.

The commander of the praetorions did try to make something of a showing, and reluctantly Honorius gave permission for patrols to be sent out to the countryside to reassure the masses that he was still in control of the situation and promise them that the savages would soon be driven out and back across the Danube.

Vergix snorted through his sweeping mustache. He was too wily not to see how deep the rot had set in among the Roman forces and their commanders. It was with regret that he reconciled himself to serving on the side he was least disposed toward. But the Norns will have their way as they weave the threads of man's existence until the time when they take their shears and snip his life. He would just have to go along with whatever it was that they had planned for him.

CHAPTER TWO

Alaric didn't understand why the Romans kept breaking their word to him. He had lived up to his end of their bargain, but time and again the Empire had shown bad faith and treachery to one who wanted to be a friend. This time they had gone too far, and he would teach them the meaning of honor if he had to march all the way to the walls of Rome itself.

When he had asked them for lands to settle his people on, the Senate had granted him territory in Moesia between the Danube and the Balkans. He knew the reason he was given permission was for his Visigoths to provide a buffer zone between the Empire and the expansions of the tribes of savage Scythia.

It was because of these tribes that he wanted to move his people out of their homelands. For three seasons there had been bad weather with small harvests. This, combined with the constant pressure of the Huns and others, led Alaric to decide that, rather than go to war when his tribes were just barely above starvation level, he would appeal to Rome.

There had been one treachery after the other. The food his people were to receive was stolen by the Roman administrators. The gold to be paid him for guarding their borders was withheld. He had needed this to pay his warriors who, while they were away from their homes guarding the frontiers, could raise no crops or cattle. The gold was necessary for them to feed their families.

Then the final stroke. During a meeting to discuss his problems, the Romans had struck without warning, killing thousands of his people including women and children. That was too much. In a rage, he had struck blindly out with his warriors, not seeking conquest, only to avenge the slaughter of his innocents.

It was to his surprise that the Roman forces opposing him fell apart under his attack. The foul deed of the Romans brought to him others who had suffered under the imperial yoke, swelling his forces with those who wanted revenge or the chance to plunder.

Alaric was no ignorant savage; he was descended from the noble house of the Balti and was an Arian Christian, as were most of his tribe. Perhaps it was the Church of Rome that caused them all this trouble. He knew the Roman church considered them heretics.

He drew much of his strength from those who were suffering under the persecution of the Church. To them he gave religious freedom. Each man to his own gods and conscience.

In the matter of war it was different. Any who came to his standards knew they had to give unquestioning obedience to him. Alaric knew that many of Rome's problems came from having too many would-be leaders all working against each other. This would not be tolerated if he was to win. There could be only one master of the armies.

All that he had ever wanted for them was to be an honored friend and ally. There was much his nation could learn from the Romans. He wanted to raise them up from being just a semi-nomadic race of warriors. He wanted cities for them and schools. All this could only come from Rome.

He gave the order. His Visigoths and their allies crossed over the frozen rivers, taking their wagons with them. One after another the cites of the Empire fell to them. Many opened their gates when they learned that those who did not oppose him would be treated gently and only their gold and the articles needed for war would be taken from them. He did not leave those he conquered to starve. He always left behind enough grain to see them through to the spring.

He would not have chosen a winter campaign, but there was no other way to get food to feed his thousands except from the granaries of Roman provinces.

Greece fell to them almost as an afterthought. Once they started moving there was no way to stop. Athens surrendered and paid tribute. Corinth and Sparta next. Then all of Argos yielded without raising arms to resist. The noble heroes of Greece were only legends, Achilles and Hector distant memories from a past that lived only in fables.

Alaric had the wealth of Greece at his disposal and distributed most of it among his tribesmen. They took slaves by the thousands, especially the women. These helped to keep the tempers of the conquerors in control. The daughters of Greece went to the wagons of their new masters, and their families were spared.

Rome put her hope in the ability of their ablest general, Stilicho, who was finally permitted to take troops from Italy and go to the aid of the Greeks. Gathering a fleet, he sailed with his army to the Isthmus, not far from Corinth.

In time he had some measure of success in repelling the barbarians who retreated slowly to the mountain of

Phloe on the border of Elis, where Stilicho put their camp under seige. But Stilicho made an error in judgment. Believing he had them bottled up and only had to wait until they were starved into submission, he left the battlefield to his subordinates in order to enjoy the fruits of his apparent victory by reveling in the sensuous pleasures of the decadent Greeks.

While Stilicho was away, Alaric outsmarted him by making a separate treaty with Arcadius, Emperor of the Eastern Roman Empire to which this part of Greece actually belonged. By making a truce, Arcadius would receive credit for ending the war, and not his cousins from Italy.

Stilicho was forced to let the Visigoths evacuate. If he had broken the treaty made with Arcadius, there might have been civil war. Thus, Alaric was able to get his warriors and their loot out of Greece safely. Stilicho returned to Italy without the victory he had gone to Greece for.

Alaric continued his negotiations with Arcadius and was given, to the astonishment of the West, the rank of Master General of Eastern Illyricum. He became the lawful master of many of the cities he had so recently plundered. They were forced to turn over their armories to him.

Night and day the forges worked to turn out arms for his warriors. Too often a Roman victory came because they were better equipped. That would be changed.

Alaric would honor his agreements with Arcadius but the memory of past treachery was too fresh for him to put much faith in it. Now he would use the time-honored ploy of playing one side against the other, all the time strengthening his armies at the expense of the two bickering empires.

Alaric had ears inside the councils of the Senate. Gold could buy much. He knew they were plotting against him again. This time he would beat them to the punch and make the first strike. He would let Italy know what it was like to be treated harshly. Then perhaps Honorius would see reason.

The armies of the Visigoths marched from Thessalonia through Pannonia into the Julian Alps. Alaric took his time, knowing his ranks would swell with swarms of volunteers who hated Rome. Over twenty-thousand men came to him who were escaped slaves and wanted a chance to hit back at their masters.

Stilicho was all that stood between Alaric and the heartland of Italy. Time and again Stilicho warded off thrusts by the Visigoths. He was shrewd and knew the mind of Alaric. He bought time with words and promises. Stilicho almost won a complete victory when he attacked the Christian Goths as they celebrated the festival of Easter. The victorious Romans took revenge on the camp of the Goths for the rape and pillage of Roman lands. Alaric withdrew back across the borders, but he would return.

Another barbarian king, Radagaisus, had invaded Gaul at the head of two-hundred thousand men from the tribes of Suevii, Vandals, Burgundians, and the Alani. His personal guard was that of twelve-thousand warriors who had distinguished themselves in combat and wore their wounds as the Romans did their badges.

Honorius left Gaul to its fate. Rome was too exhausted to do more than defend her own territorial borders. While Alaric rested, Radagaisus marched. He laid waste all before him, and crossed from Gaul into Italy with such speed that he had the city of Florence under siege before any effective resistance could be mounted against him. He was only a hundred and eighty miles from Rome, and all that stood in his way was a hastily gathered force under the command of Stilicho.

Stilicho had waited until the barbarians were fully

involved with their siege of Milan. He knew the effect that long sieges had, not only on the defenders, but also on an attacking force. He estimated correctly the amount of time it would take for the invaders to use up their supplies and their gleanings from the countryside, then he struck. He had managed to put together nearly thirty legions, of which a large number were from tribes still allied more to him personally than to Rome. He surrounded the weakened and hungry force of Radagaisus and took him prisoner. About a hundred-thousand warriors managed to escape to the valleys between the Appomonnia and the Danube. There they licked their wounds and waited.

Radagaisus was executed by order of Honorius, and Stilicho was, for the second time, awarded the title of Savior of Rome. Stilicho was the most respected Roman the Empire had, and even the barbarians from a dozen tribes paid him his due as a war chieftain and leader. He even made a treaty with Alaric, in which Alaric was again given command of Roman territory as a governor. This assured, for the time being anyway, a period of relative peace, in which the Roman forces could be rebuilt and new legions formed.

Stilicho, unfortunately, became too popular. Honorius became jealous and listened to the lies told him by one Olympius, a young, ambitious toady who curried favor with Honorius by telling him what he most wanted to hear. Stilicho was driven to take refuge in a church in Ravenna where he claimed sanctuary, but even this was denied when Count Heraclian tricked Stilicho into coming outside the confines of the church. The Bishop of Ravenna had been assured by Heraclian that he only wanted to put Stilicho under arrest, but when Stilicho came forth, the Count immediately produced another document ordering his immediate execution. Stilicho went to his death nobly and bared his neck to the executioner's blade without any protest or plea for mercy.

Rome's last great general was dead. There was no one left in the empire to hold back the gathering storm on the frontiers.

Alaric was not long in coming. The death of Stilicho had removed the last great obstacle from his path and he moved into Italy, again gathering to him the warriors that escaped the slaughter of Radagaisus, and even the tribesmen that fought so valiantly for Rome under the leadership of Stilicho came to him and added another thirty-thousand hard men to his standards.

Casca and Vergix killed time in Ravenna on guard details and escort duty for the Emperor, who decided to stay behind the high walls of Ravenna rather than return to Rome. He was much safer here than in the eternal city. Alaric marched south, leaving Ravenna alone. He wasn't going to make the same mistake that Radagaisus had and tie down his men in a long exhausting siege. He was after the greater prize—Rome itself—and would not be denied it this time.

City after city fell to him—Aquileia, Altinum, Concordia and Cremona. He marched along the coast of the Adriatic, using the roads built by Rome to transport his own legions along the Falminian Way by passing Narni. The Goths pitched their tents outside the walls of Rome. At the court of Ravenna, Honorius continued his life-style and luxury, but in his capitol, the ravens of death had gathered.

Casca knew what the word siege meant—starvation and disease, hardship to such a degree that the average person would readily perform acts he would never have thought himself capable of.

Nothing entered the gates of Rome. The food stopped and those inside came face to face with the worst nightmare in the six-hundred-year history of the city.

Alaric required neighboring states to provide his forces with regular shipments of supplies and made no further moves. He was now going to try and consolidate his gains and take over actual control of what remained of the Roman Empire and he still accepted delegations from Honorius showing them courtesy and restraint in his demands. He knew that the counselors of Honorius were looking for any sign of weakness on his part and that wishful thinking and the need to reinforce the image would force them to try and take advantage of him.

He waited, and it wasn't long in coming that Honorius, at the urging of Olympius, ordered six thousand of his Dalmations to march to Rome, right through the lands occupied by the Goths and their allies. Casca and Vergix were ordered to go along with them as part of a small contingent of his Imperial Guard to show the Emperor's colors in Rome.

They never reached the gates. The six thousand under the command of Valens died under the lances and blades of fifty-thousand Goths and Huns. Only Valens with a hundred soldiers escaped the slaughter; the rest lay broken on the fields and the few survivors were being herded off to slave pens.

Casca and Vergix marched with them. Vergix had a broken arm and Casca showed several cuts on his already well-marked hide. He had been knocked unconscious by a thrown axe that nearly split his helmet open and Vergix had stood over his body fighting like a madman until he was so exhausted he could barely stand. His arm was broken by a club-wielding Vandal.

When Vergix fell, he raised his face and called to Father Odin with what he thought would be his last breath. That was what saved him. The Vandal halted in midair what was to be Vergix's death blow.

"Are you of the tribes?"

Vergix avowed as how he was and that he was ready to die. A Goth officer rode up at that time and asked what the matter was and when told Vergix was German, he gave the Vandal orders to take him prisoner. Alaric wished for all men from the tribes found in Roman uniform to be brought to him. As Casca was unconscious and of fair enough coloring to pass, Vergix told them he, too, was of the tribes. Therefore, Casca was permitted to survive this day and was taken from the field chained by the neck, marching along with several hundred others, but kept apart from them.

Casca's head throbbed for three days and spots of many colors danced before his eyes, partially from the knock on the head and partially from hunger. They were not fed until the tents of Alaric came into sight. They were hustled off to a separate pen where they were held with a number of other Goths, Vandals, Marcomanni, and Suevii that had been found bearing the arms of Rome. The rest of the captive legionnaires disappeared over a rise.

In Rome, the daily dole of three pounds of bread was cut again and again, until there was nothing to be given out to the masses. The rich continued to feed themselves on delicacies and rare vintages for a time, believing that relief was sure to come soon, but the weeks rolled by and they too began to feel the gnawing fear of desperate hunger. Their wealth was spent on buying morsels to eat that they would have cast to their dogs before, and they bid over a piece of half-decayed horse flesh as if it were a priceless work of art.

Casca knew that some were even now feeding on the flesh of humans. And with starvation came disease and corpses filled the streets; the pungent odor of death hung over the city, heavy and nauseating.

Pomiamus, Prefect of Rome, even considered resorting to spells and sacrifices that would bring down the barbarians, but the religious wail of the Christians claimed this was too close to profanation and the sacrifices never took place. Instead, when faith in the Emperor's promises failed, Pomiamus had no choice but to ask for mercy from the Gothic prince. When Pomiamus's delegation, led by Basilius, a Senator of ancient origin, was admitted into the presence of Alaric, they tried to bluff their way by declaring that if Alaric didn't want to give them fair and easy terms, he would have to face an armed populace in all its righteous rage.

Alaric, knowing the true state of the inhabitants of the now less than immortal city, replied, "The thicker the hay, the easier it's mowed." He then explained the degree of his knowledge of the city and its capabilities to defend itself. Alaric watched the Romans, knowing he had them by the short hairs.

He smiled as he told them that in exchange for not leveling the walls of Rome, all he wanted was all the gold and silver in the city, no matter who it belonged to, and everything of value that could be moved or torn down.

The senator asked in despair, "Then what do you plan on leaving us?"

Alaric laughed harshly. "Your lives."

Alaric knew that he couldn't get everything he

wanted, as much would be hidden that he could never recover and the time it would take to do a complete job of pillaging the city was more than he wanted to stay in the region. He needed new grounds to forage from. So he made his final offer and accepted a payment of five thousand pounds of gold, thirty of silver, four thousand robes of silk—which were worth their weight in gold—and three thousand pounds of pepper from India.

Alaric was content for the moment, and as agreed, he gave the orders for his tribes to form, leaving the city walls, moving into the more prosperous countryside of Tuscany where he could set up his winter camp with the assurance there would be no starvation among his own people, which had grown by another forty thousand barbarian slaves that had broken free from their masters and joined his standard. Also from the north, he received a reinforcement of Goths and Huns brought to him by Ataulf, the brother of his wife. Alaric had the spirit of a barbarian chieftain and the discipline of a Roman general of Caesar and his name was enough to cause fear the length of Italia, for none knew when he might choose to move again.

Alaric was kept well-informed in intelligence matters. When he received word that two tribesmen wearing the armor of the praetorians had been captured, he ordered them into his presence. Praetorians could tell him much about the inner workings of Honorius's court.

Casca and Vergix were herded into Alaric's tent and forced to their knees until they were given permission to rise. Casca stood, still wearing the gold-trimmed armors of the guards, as did Vergix.

Alaric was silent for a moment watching them

through his bright, clear blue eyes. He spoke first to Vergix, "How came you to be wearing the arms of Rome?"

Vergix told him straightforwardly the story of his and Casca's day in the arena and the promise they had to give in order to be freed.

Alaric nodded. "And have you been true to your oath of loyalty to him?"

Vergix spoke firmly, with no quiver in his voice. "I have."

Alaric turned to Casca, eyeing him up and down. "You are not of the tribes, though you have lighter hair and eyes than most Latins. There is a mannerism to you that speaks of Rome. The way you stand is that of a soldier of the legions. I know that you are not of my kinsmen because even here the tale of the fight you and this one made in the arena of Ravenna has come to be known. But no matter, did you also keep your oath of loyalty to Honrius?"

Casca faced Alaric, answering him as one soldier would to another, "Yes, an oath is not lightly broken, even if it is given under pressure."

Alaric called for wine and indicated for the two to join him at a table. He liked the looks of these two. Pouring for all three, he spoke again, "If you had said otherwise, or if I believed you had lied, your heads would now be looking for their bodies. It is good that you were loyal while in the service of Honorius, weak and dishonorable though he may be. But now you are no longer under his authority, but mine. I have no desire to kill those that might be useful to me; therefore, if I grant you your lives, will you serve me as well?"

Vergix took his time answering, hiding his thoughts behind his wine cup. A wrong answer meant death.

Was he being tested again? He made up his mind. "Aye, Lord Alaric, I will serve. I can be of no use to Honorius now. You have my head in your hands and if you decide to take it, then surely I could be of no further use to the Romans. My oath was only given in order to save my life. I did that once and surely there could be no more dishonor if I did it again under the same circumstances."

Alaric laughed deeply. "So be it, your head shall remain on your shoulders. And you, Roman, will you also swear fealty to me?"

Casca knew his answer and didn't have to wait before making it. "No, lord, I cannot give you that oath."

"And why not?" Alaric watched him.

Casca stood at attention, picking his words carefully.

"I know the days of Rome's greatness are passing, that she may never rise again, but still I cannot be a party to the slaughter of those of my own race—though it must surely come if not this day then another. I know that a new dawn is rising and perhaps it is time for Rome to be allowed to die, but I have been her son too long to help kill her, even to stop the rot that has set in."

Alaric was not displeased at the response. "That is a good answer, Roman, and I respect you for it. Loyalty to a lost cause may be foolhardy, but it is noble. You have both pleased me this evening and I give you your lives. You"—indicating Vergix—"shall join my forces among your brothers. You"—to Casca—"shall be allowed to live, but make no mistake. It shall be only as long as you don't interfere with my plans. If I kept you in chains you would not be able to help Rome. I would prefer to put bonds on you of a lighter kind. Will you give me your oath not to betray me? If you do, there will be no chains other than those of your own honor. But if you give your oath and lie, then not only you but your friend shall pay for it in a manner that shall have you screaming for weeks."

Casca considered his choice and gave his oath not to interfere. Alaric kept him under close watch for a few days, though Vergix was given complete freedom of movement.

There was nothing Casca could do but wait and watch the events that were coming; he knew there could only be one end at this stage.

It came soon. Alaric took the attempt of the Dalmations to reach Rome as a breach of faith, and moved on the city again. As winter was on them, he took first the port of Ostia from which all grain had to be shipped by barges up the Tiber. With this single move, he once more had Rome at his mercy and the specter of famine again struck the city.

The gates of Rome were opened to Alaric by those who wished to curry favor for themselves. He occupied the city and proclaimed a senator named Attalus the Emperor, which was rapidly ratified by the Senate. Alaric knew that he could never unite all Italy behind him unless he had an acceptable figurehead, and Attalus was of a respected and noble family.

Things went well enough for a time, but fortune smiled on Honorius, who received reinforcements and gold from Africa through the able hands of Count Heraclian. He broke agreements time and again, violating their truce with Alaric and the fickle population of Rome removed the purple from the shoulders of Attalus.

For the third time, Alaric came to the city, but this time there would be no saving it. The Salerian Gate was opened for him by his agents and the Goths poured into Rome with a vengeance. This time they were to take what they wanted from the city and its people. The only places given protection were those of worship; they were not to be touched.

Casca stood with Alaric and Vergix as the Goths entered the Salerian Gates. He saw the first flame lick up to the night sky. One thousand sixty-three years after her founding, Rome was being sacked, a fate she had given to innumerable other cities.

Alaric watched his captive. He understood the emotions going through him. He told Casca sadly, "There is no other way. Rome has to be cleansed that a new order may be founded. I will not kill Rome, only cut off the diseased parts."

A troop of two thousand Vandals poured through the gates which were now in flames. "We do not have much time to speak. I will be needed soon, but understand this. I have long admired the accomplishments of your nation. If I can infuse the vitality of my tribesmen with the culture and knowledge of Rome, there could come a new order which could hold the world together for centuries. But before that can take place, an example has to be made. Rome has to learn to accept and obey. Thousands will die, but that is a small price to pay for what both sides will win if I succeed. Between us we will become one people so powerful, both in arms and knowledge, that no one could ever stand against us. The days of the Roman Republic will be brought back."

Casca took a deep breath and let the air out slowly.

"You know what I say is true, Roman. This day be glad it is I and not the King of the Huns whose men are riding through those gates."

Casca's eyes were stinging both from smoke and emotion as he replied, "I know that what you are saying is true, but still the knowing and the seeing are two different things and it hurts me to watch my city die."

Vergix shifted, uncomfortable at the conversation. His was a simpler mind. He wanted to be in on the looting, but he did not wish to offend his friend.

Alaric signaled for one of his officers to come to him. The Goth saluted with drawn sword.

"Take this man to Ostia. He is to be put on board the first ship out to any port other than one of Italy." He put a leather pouch of coins in Casca's hand. "Go away from me and this place. There is nothing for you here but pain and nothing you can do to help anyone. Perhaps I will succeed in my dream, perhaps not. That is in the hands of fate. All I can do is to follow my wyrd and you can do no less yourself. Go away from me, Roman! You give me too much pain, for I see myself in your eyes and it is not good for a man to look too closely at himself. Go away, Roman, go away."

Casca obeyed and followed after the Gothic officer after saying farewell to Vergix. The two rode away from the flames of Rome. He never looked back. In some ways he hoped Alaric would be successful, but he was a dreamer and dreams seldom come true.

For six days the rape of Rome continued. Nobles found themselves on their knees serving food and drink to Goths and Scythians, watching as the barbarians took their pleasure with their daughters and wives. They could do nothing to protest or to stop it.

Rome had to be taught a hard lesson. Alaric had the fires put out after the first night. He would not have the city burned to the ground, but all that was in it belonged to his men. They could not be denied their rights a third time.

He had two hundred of his own men beheaded for

disobeying him and starting fires. As a rule, the barbarians were merciful when not provoked by resistance. But any who stood between them and what they wanted was silenced in his protests with an ax or sword.

On the seventh day, Alaric gave the order for the plundering to cease. He was obeyed. His wagons were loaded with the spoils of Rome. Gold and silver statues were melted down for easier handling. Furniture and clothing, anything that was of value, was taken and this time the secret hoards of the rich were found when tongues were loosened with red hot irons.

Only one senator lost his life at the hands of a Goth. The rest of the nobility, though treated roughly, were given their lives and ransomed at modest prices.

There was nothing left for the barbarians in Rome. They went back into the country, passing thousands of panic-stricken citizens who had fled the city. These they ignored. They already had more spoils than they could count and the few pitiful possessions of the refugees were of no interest to them. Ten thousand slaves were taken with them just to haul the wagons and carry on their backs the wealth of Rome.

Alaric watched it all from his horse. Now perhaps Honorius would be ready to listen to reason and there could be made a new beginning that would benefit them all.

CHAPTER THREE

Dry winds blew clouds of dust skywards. In the pre-dawn light, it looked as if the skies were weeping through a shaded veil of blood. Stretching back farther than the eye could see, the tribes and the nations of the Hun were on the move.

Ch'ing Lie kept to the flanks, bypassing the warriors. No one paid him any heed. He was just one man alone and no threat to the power of the Huns. Ch'ing Li, former minister to the Emperor of the Dragon throne of the Eastern Chin, did not look the part he had played for many years as an imperial advisor. Gone were the robes of fine silk and pavilions filled with the softness of beautiful women and the rarest of viands. Gone were the rings of gold and jade as was his seal of office, the Chu hou wang. Now he was wearing only rags covered with filth and dust to protect his thin—almost maidenly— body from the elements.

But under his robes, carefully wrapped in a covering of oiled waterproof silk, was the key to new fortune and power. There was only one man he could take it to that might understand what it meant and put it and him to use . . . Attila.

Several times he had been halted by patrols of the

King of the Huns, but, as always, when he said he was a messenger from Chin, they permitted him to pass, after a gift of a few coins to prove that he was not a beggar and therefore fair game for their pleasure. When he ran out of coins, he showed them the scroll wrapped in its precious silk.

The Huns were an ignorant people who were still mystified by the fact that words and messages could be made with squiggles on paper. But his manner, though his clothes were poor, was that of one used to power. They let him pass.

Ch'ing Li halted his weary horse on a rise. Shading his eyes with a thin, blue-veined hand, he looked to the west. There he could see his goal—a number of tents on high ground with a ring of warriors around them facing outwards, weapons in their hands. Near the tents were set the standards of the Huns. The horse and yak tails of the western and eastern tribes mingled with those of the Alani, whose standards were the skulls of their enemies, set on tall poles.

There were over fifty tall poles around the tents. That meant that Attila and his brother, Bleda, were having a meeting with his Toumans, Cur-quans and chieftains. Where the standards were, so were the leaders. He kicked his animal into a half-hearted gallop.

As he heard the ring of armed warriors, he reined his horse to a standstill. Fifty archers had their bows aimed at him, the strings drawn back to their ears. A thick-bodied warrior wearing armor made of bone scales came to him.

Ch'ing Li got his first good look at a Cur-quan of the Huns. Harmatta was near the age of fifty though he wasn't sure of his birth date himself. His upper lip was graced with a long wispy mustache. His features looked as if the artist designing him had gotten tired and left the work only half finished. The cheekbones were too high and thick, the nose flattened at the bridge making the nostrils flare out. His face has been seared with hot irons in his infancy, and the nose was flattened at birth by having a band tied over its bridge to spread it out so that the nasal guard of a helmet would better fit him.

In his face Ch'ing Li thought he could barely make out some other bloodlines. The hair under the bell-shaped helmet had dirty yellow streaks mixed in with the gray, and the eyes had an off-blue cast to them, nearly gray. On his arms were bands of gold set with enough gems to buy a dozen handsome slave girls of Egypt.

When he spoke it was in the tongue of the Kurtigur. Ch'ing Li had planned for this event. When he had first been sent into exile from the courts of Chin, he had been taken to the Jade Gate and thrust out into the wilds. He barely managed to reach the oasis town of Ho t'ien near the great wastes of the Tkla-Makan.

There he had stayed, using the small gems he had sewn into the lining of his robes to provide the bare necessities of life. While in that desolate and crude trading post and halfway house for those traveling the Silk Road, he decided upon the course he would take and the necessity of meeting the King of the Huns.

To prepare for this, he purchased, at a very reasonable cost, a slave who knew their tongue. He forced himself to learn the animal guttural sibilants that served the Hun as speech. His slave had died five weeks earlier when they had run short of food and water. His slave was not a good provider; therefore, he was of no use. Ch'ing Li poisoned him, leaving the corpse to dry in the sun of the high desert.

Harmatta spoke again, "What do you wish here, dog? Can you not see this is the camp of Attila?"

Ch'ing Li threw back the cowl of his hooded robe, showing his face. There was no fear in the brown eyes behind their heavy-lidded epicanthic folds. Only calm, cold intelligence showed through them.

Harmatta knew this man was not a beggar, neither was he a warrior. Ch'ing Li worked his tongue around the uncomfortable speech of the Huns replying slowly, "I come as a messenger to the Lord Attila, that and no more."

Harmatta spoke again, stepping out of the line of warriors until he was near enough to the stranger to haul him off his horse. "I am Harmatta, Hetman of the Kutrigur and servant to the Master. I will take your message to our Lord."

Ch'ing Li repeated himself in the same manner and tone. "I come as a messenger to the Lord Attila, none other may hear the message I bear."

Harmatta chewed at the end of his mustache. The man was not afraid of him. For one to demand to speak to Attila and no other meant that he must have important information or else he was a fool who wished to have his spirit join those of his ancestors. This little man did not look or sound like a fool.

Others from the compound gathered to hear the conversation. Several enjoyed Harmatta's discomfort in dealing with the imperturbable little weakling. Among them was the elder son of Attila, Arnak, looking like a younger version of Harmatta. Beside him was Ongesh, first adviser to Attila and Master of the Commissary. Both wore armor of the style favored in Constantinople, richly embossed, decorated with designs of silver and gold.

Arnak whispered in Ongesh's ear and the councilor left him to enter the tent of their master. Harmatta was still trying to convince Ch'ing Li to give him some idea as to the content of his message or at least who he had come from, when there came a hush over the compound. Only the guards remained standing on their feet. All others fell to their faces on the dust before the man who had come out of his tent.

Attila, son of Mundzuk, Touman of the Thousand Tribes, was watching them. Nobles and common warriors, heroes and wise men, all fell to their faces in the presence of Attila. Even his own son placed his face to the earth, knowing that not to pay proper respect as did the others could mean that his head would leave his body, depending on the mood of his father. There were no favorites where true power walked.

Harmatta followed suit when he knew that Attila was present. The only one who didn't was Ch'ing Li, who dismounted and walked slowly toward Attila.

Attila pointed at him with an extended forefinger. Ch'ing Li obeyed the unspoken command and did as the others. In the face of the Master of the Huns, he saw his death if he didn't instantly obey. He buried his face in the dry earth, waiting. . . .

Of all the nobles, only Ongesh was permitted to stand in the presence of Attila. A short barking command from him and all were permitted to rise.

Ch'ing Li got back to his feet, standing still. Attila spoke quietly a few words that Ch'ing Li couldn't make out and Harmatta answered, "Lord, this one claims to be a messenger, but—"

His explanation was cut short by Attila's upraised hand. Silence! Attila walked over to them. With every step, Ch'ing Li knew he had chosen correctly to come to this place. If only he could survive the next few minutes. The Master of the Huns exuded raw primal power.

Attila wore none of the riches of his officers, no arm

bands of precious gold. No rare gems set in rings of electrum. He wore only a plain, well-used sheepskin jacket with the hair to the outside to cover his barrel chest. A wide belt of red copper encircled the thick muscles of his waist. In the belt was a long dagger of plain workmanship.

It was the face that told Ch'ing Li the story. Eyes dark, cold, controlled and very intelligent. He wore his hair in a single scalp lock set on the right side of his head to hang over his shoulder. Ch'ing Li knew the control Attila was showing was of the enforced kind and one not to his nature. There was raw brutal power and violence lying behind the heavy eyelids.

Attila looked him over, missing nothing from foot to crown. He saw everything about the man from Chin. Turning his back he spoke again quietly, every syllable dripping with intensity, "Bring this man to my tent." Attila strode back to his quarters leaving the rest of those outside to heave sighs of relief that none had died.

Ch'ing Li started to follow but was halted by the guards who searched him for weapons, removing even the thin blade he used for eating. One of them found the scroll in its wrapping and started to unroll it. Ch'ing Li snatched it back from the hands of the Hun and nearly lost his life in the doing as a thick sword blade touched his throat.

He was stopped from being killed by a single word from Harmatta who took the scroll from him, looked it over and gave it back.

Ch'ing Li was shaking with relief when they permitted him to enter the tent of Attila. Ongesh stood at the flap to the black felt structure, holding it open. Ch'ing Li hesitated. "What I have is for the ears of Attila alone." He paused, waiting.

Ongesh's face paled a little but then he waved him on inside and closed the flap, remaining outside.

Ch'ing Li remained in the tent for several hours. What went on inside or what Ch'ing Li said to the Master was never known, but when the flap opened, he and Attila came forth. There was a glint in the eyes of Attila that had a hungry look to it.

He raised his voice so all could hear clearly. "By my command this man, Ch'ing Li, is to be shown honor. He is given the rank of Cur-quan. He is to be permitted to visit me at any time of the day or night without hindrance. This is my word, let it be done."

Ch'ing Li was taken to a nearby tent and shown inside. The previous owner of it had been told to get out. He only nodded his head, took his weapons and left, leaving all else there for the tent's new master. Losing his tent wasn't important; he would merely go to Ongesh and be given a new one from the wagons.

In the shade of the black tent, Ch'ing Li let loose of his control. Sitting down on a cushion, his body started shaking with the release of his emotions. He had won! It had been a gamble that he would even be received by the Master of the Huns. It was true that he did come as a messenger, not one from a distant king, but as his own. He bore with him the scroll as his talisman. In it was the secret to power such as the Hun had never dreamed of.

The scroll contained the writings of Sun Tz'u and the collected wisdom of the wars of Chin for over five hundred years. The scroll contained it all—tactics and strategy, the manner in which to use your enemy's mind against him, when to move your forces and where to stay and fight. It was all there in Tz'u's *The Art of War*. With the armies of Attila for tools and he to advise, there would be nothing that could stand in their way.

The armies of Attila would one day help him to gain his revenge on those who had betrayed him, forcing him to leave the court of the Son of Heaven. When he returned, it would be at the head of an army such as the world had never known before. But first they would have to move West. It was there he could gather the wealth and manpower from the nations he would subject, then he would return to the great wall and over it. The scroll of *The Art of War* was his secret weapon and the Huns would be his sword.

Ch'ing Li soon found out that as a councilor of the Master, there was little he could wish for that was not given. The large two-wheeled wains of the Huns were a veritable cornucopia containing everything from fine silks to the most common of items.

The warrior he displaced came to him later to present himself as the commander of the new Cur-quan's escort and bodyguard. He identified himself as Basich-cur, commander of thirty warriors for his new master's service.

Ch'ing Li was feeling much better about the turn of his fortune as bath water was heated, much to the amazement of the Huns, in large copper pots used by them for the boiling of mutton or whatever else they chose to eat. After the luxury of a hot bath, he dressed in clean robes of polychrome silk brought from the wagons for his approval. He was most positively feeling quite good about his decision to come to this place.

He had been right in his judgments so far; however, he might have to reevaluate his previous ideas about the Hun leader, Attila. He was not a fool or an ignorant savage. Ch'ing learned from their meeting that Attila had spent much time as a hostage at the courts of both Rome and Constantinople. He was a savage, yes, but not a fool.

Attila had listened to him without speaking for an hour, letting Ch'ing Li explain what he had to offer. Then Ch'ing Li had spent the next three hours answering questions about what should be done under certain circumstances and conditions.

The answers given Attila pleased him, he could use the delicate man from Chin and would. He made no promises of either reward or punishment; it was unnecessary. Ch'ing Li understood perfectly his arrangement— serve Attila well and live with all that he desired in the way of wealth and slaves, or fail him and die most horribly. There were no other conditions.

Once he was properly attired as was befitting his new rank, he followed after Basich-cur to inspect his body-guard. He was impressed by the complete acceptance of Attila's power. Basich-cur showed no sign of irritation at being evicted. The only thing of importance to him was to do that which his Master wished.

Basich-cur led Ch'ing to where he found himself facing thirty fierce warriors of the tribe of the Utigur. They, like their Oylan-cur, would obey without hesitation orders from Attila, even to slitting the throats of their own fathers. This was to be his personal guard. Most were men in their thirties with the marks of war on them, hard men who rode under the blue horsetailed standard of the Utigurs. All were well armed and most had fair armor of one sort or another to cover them. As he inspected them, he made intelligent comments about one or the other of the warriors pertaining to their weapons or horses. When he had finished his inspection, he congratulated Basich-cur on the good condition of the men and animals in his charge.

He knew the way to a leader's heart was through his men, his valor or his horsemanship. The observations he made proved to Basich-cur that he knew what he was talking about and would give him respect in his eyes and those of the Oylan.

That evening he dined in the tent of Attila. Present were two of Attila's sons, the elder Ellac and his brother Arnak. Ch'ing Li wondered where Attila's brother, Bleda, was.

Ongesh stood close by his master. He gave him a look that was neither friendly nor hostile. He would have to be careful not to step on that one's toes.

Harmatta was there and given a favored place near Attila where he could watch all the others' faces. Harmatta, he found out, was not only the father of one of Attila's favorite wives, he was also the chief shaman of the tribes. It was he who would read the portents of the heavens by the movements of the stars or scrape the membrane away from the shoulder blade of a sheep or ox to interpret the cracks in the bone once it had been placed on a fire until it swelled and cracked. In these cracks, the future could be read by the manner in which they split the bone.

In all there were over thirty other leaders present— from blood members of the clans to those that had been conquered and absorbed into the horde. Among these were the fierce headhunting Alans who were taller than their Hunnish cousins and fairer of skin and hair but were second to none in the pleasures they took from the letting of blood or plunder. Dark-faced Ulgers, the Cur-quan of the Unugar, sat beside the Hetman of the Sabiri, another conquered race that now took the name of Hun for themselves with pride.

Then there was the Touman of the proud Saraguri which destroyed more than a hundred tribes before they were taken by Attila and made into his loyal vassals. There were others in this warlike company who represented the strength of the tribes and those peoples subject to them.

Among the predominately dark-haired, brown-eyed chieftains, he saw several men of huge size with yellow or red hair who kept massive axes or extremely long, heavy swords between their legs. Ch'ing Li didn't think he could have raised one of the swords with both hands, much less one. These were the newest of the allies that had come to Attila. Their speech was even more guttural and barbaric-sounding than that of the Huns. They were the Gepidae and their distant cousins the Goths, peoples unknown to Ch'ing Li.

Men of that size and strength would be invaluable. He would learn more about them later. They reminded him of one he had heard of in the service of the Emperor Tzin over fifty years ago. They looked a great deal like the description he had heard of the large, big-nosed foreigner who led the armies of the Emperor back then. The foreigner had won great victories for the Dragon Throne; then one day rode off, never to be seen again. But it was said he was a terrible warrior who had been touched by the gods with great powers.

He would be known by the scar that ran from the corner of his eye to his mouth. It was said he had eyes of blue-gray. But that would do him no good here. Even if the man were still alive and sitting across from him, he wouldn't be able to recognize him, for many of the big noses here had the same marks on them and the same odd ugly coloration in their eyes.

Ch'ing Li was careful not to contribute too much to the conversations taking place. It would be best if he spoke only when asked something directly and then make the questioner think he thought of the answer. He would be the shadow of Attila. Let the others claim the glory; he would know who was in control. When the time came, he would assert himself, but now was the time to make friends, if that was possible, with these foul-smelling creatures.

He would be polite and properly impressed by the vulgarians who seemed only to delight in the numbers of men they had butchered or the women they had raped. Animals! Disgusting brutes, but they would be useful.

As he planned, he was the shadow by the ear of Attila, whispering in it while others stormed and raged. It was he who made Attila understand that Bleda would have to go, leaving him the sole master of the Huns. He had never laid eyes on the brother of Attila who commanded the western part of the Hunnish lands, but he knew that there had to come a time when they would be in conflict. He had to have only one in command and he had chosen. Bleda must die!

It didn't take much for Attila to see the wisdom of his advice pertaining to a body with two heads. Attila said nothing, but Ch'ing Li could see the wheels turning in his mind. He was pleased when less than a month later, the word had come that Bleda had died of poison.

Attila made his mind up fast, and besides, he had never liked his older brother much anyway. When they were children, Bleda had always teased and mocked the younger Attila.

The changes Ch'ing Li made in the plans of the Huns brought them wealth they didn't even have to fight for. He taught them how to use the time-honored method of the implied threat. From this time forward, he would direct them in long-range planning, something the Hun never worried about before.

The year now by the Roman reckoning was 434 Anno Domini. Attila and his brother had been in power less than two years after the death of their uncle, Ruga.

They had turned the Huns into a force to be reckoned with in a remarkably short time. The Huns had existed as a partially united nation only, since the first true King of the Huns, Kara-ton, had united the tribes of the Kutrigur and Utiger.

Now Attila was the sole leader. He had been in total control now for two years and had accomplished more in that time than had been achieved in the last forty.

Ch'ing Li taught him the reasons for the unconscious successes of the Huns. How their movements of sixty years earlier had forced the Ostrogoths to move across the Dniester and pressured the Visigoths of Athanaris to go into Roman Pannonia. But the bulk of the Visigoths had appeared on the lower Danube after being beaten in battle by the Huns. They had appealed to Rome for permission to settle in Dacia. This was permitted by Emperor Valens who saw them as a buffer against the expanding power of the Hun. But the corruption among Roman officials, who were supposed to supply the Visigoths with food until they could gather a harvest, forced them to go to war in order to avoid starvation.

When the Visigoths attacked, they were joined by others who had become disillusioned with the lies and corruption of Rome. To the strength of the Visigoths was added that of the Ostrogoths of Saphrax and Altheus. Many of their men, who had been serving under the standards of Rome, returned to their tribes.

There was even a loose alliance with few independent tribes of the Huns and Alans who wanted in on the plunder. Several Roman armies were defeated in rapid succession which encouraged even more barbarians to join them, until they finally engaged the largest army yet fielded against them at a place called Ad Salice in the Dorogea. The Romans were slaughtered almost to a man. The date would long be remembered as a day of shame for the Romans. It was the ninth of August 378.

After this humiliation of Roman arms, Emperor Valens took command himself of a large force and met the Visigoths near Adrianopole. Two-thirds of his army was wiped out and he was killed in the battle. All of these events led to the final humiliation of Rome and the eventual sacking of the city itself. The rot in Rome had gone too far to be cured quickly enough to resist the more vital peoples of the savage nations.

After the looting of Rome, the barbarians showed no desire to inherit the mantle of civilization and accepted a huge bribe of gold to leave most of Italy. But it was too late to do the diminished and splintered Empire any good. Rome could be taken by the Huns, and where the barbarians of the Germanic tribes had no idea of how to administer a civilized culture, he, Ch'ing Li, did.

For the next ten years, the security of Rome rested on the swords of the barbarians. Alaric's successor, Ataulf, took the sister of Honorius as his bride. He tried to keep the empire together with Honorius as a puppet emperor. But when he died there was no one to take his place and the Germans themselves became disjointed; it was each tribe for itself.

During this time the Roman general, Flavius Constantius, reorganized what remained of the Western Empire and rebuilt much of its armies. He married the widow of Ataulf, the sister of Honorius, and proclaimed himself co-Emperor in 421. He died before the year was out under suspicious circumstances. It was shortly after this that the first Hunnish attacks came to Roman provinces.

For the next twenty years, constant harassments kept the Romans on edge and unable to mount an effective counterforce as they were faced with massive problems from Gaul to Africa. It was too much for the depleted resources of the Western Empire to deal with. Rome had to add increasingly more numbers of barbarians to the ranks of the federati and even the legions to fill out their ranks.

All of these conditions said the time was right for a new power to make its appearance. And while the name in the mouths of the conquered people would be Attila, it would be Ch'ing Li who pulled the strings.

Ch'ing Li would read the signs as no other. From the first days with the Huns he had begun to acquire information from captives and traders, until he knew more of the workings of Rome, its alliances and weaknesses than most of those who sat in the powerless Roman Senate and dreamed of the glory of bygone years.

The time was right, the place was here, and he had the means. Soon he would have it all. He made sacrifices to the spirits of his ancestors to ask their aid in this magnificent venture. He was very much pleased.

Attila had his reasons to be pleased as well. They had made good progress since Ch'ing had come to the Huns. His first main coup was the Treaty of Margius, where he forced the Eastern Romans to double their payment of gold to the Huns to seven hundred pounds a year. Ch'ing needed this to buy arms and equipment that the Huns couldn't make for themselves. He was letting the Romans pay for the outfitting of the forces that would destroy them.

His next move was to convince Attila to leave the Romans alone for a time and secure his own lands by subduing the tribes that had not yet sworn allegiance to him. It would not do to have enemies inside your own borders when you were waging a major war elsewhere. In addition, by absorbing the tribes of the steppes, he would then add the numbers of their warriors to his own forces, increasing the supply of manpower he could call on by two- or three-fold.

In the Roman year 440, the Empire didn't make its payment of gold and it was time to test their new war machine. Ch'ing had Attila wait until the Romans were occupied with troubles on their eastern and western borders; then he made a heavy raid on the provinces of the Danubian frontier. In rapid succession, they captured and destroyed the major cities of Viminacium, Sirmium, Singidunum and a dozen lesser towns.

Ch'ing convinced Attila to accept a truce with Rome in 442 for a couple of reasons: the Hunnish forces need to rest and regroup; and the Romans had pulled back their armies from the west and were now in strength. Ch'ing did not want his new tool to be damaged. Timing was everything.

His hardest task was not winning battles but keeping Attila restrained from listening to his warlords who only wanted to fight endlessly, or his filthy seers who were envious of his influence. Because Ch'ing had been right in his judgments so far, Attila gave in to him when he presented his arguments.

The Huns were not ready for an all-out war with Rome. But soon they would be. The small victories they had won at little cost to themselves would give the newly absorbed tribes of their lands confidence and a desire to participate as willing allies of their masters.

The next year, Ch'ing waited for the right time to move again. Attila moved his warriors against Ratiaria on the Danube and rushed into the interior toward Nasissu and Sedica, bypassing most strongholds and striking to the rear. After wasting both of these major cities, he turned toward Constantinople, sacked Philopolis and for the first time defeated a major Roman army commanded by the *praetor militarium,* Aspar, in a series of fast-moving battles in which the greater mobility of his horse archers wore the Roman forces out in a campaign of maneuver.

Ch'ing knew there was not any way for them to breach the walls of Constantinople, but that was never his intent. He knew the effect that just the thought of having the fierce savage warriors of the steppes near them would have. His real goal was the successful attack on the mind of the enemy, not the taking of burned-out cities which they couldn't hold.

Ch'ing had Attila turn from the capital of the Eastern Romans to destroy the remaining Roman forces in the field which had withdrawn into the narrow peninsula of Gallipoli. Time was pressing him but they had reached the sea both south and north of Constantinople.

His next move was to use the threat of Hun occupation to force their opponents who were sitting behind the great walls in terror to make a new treaty quickly. If the Eastern Romans had held out. Ch'ing would have had to have advised Attila to leave without one as there would soon be a shortage of food for his men. They couldn't stay in the field much longer.

The Eastern Romans were more than willing to meet his terms to make a payment of six thousand pounds of gold immediately and to increase their yearly tribute to two thousand pounds.

Ch'ing had accomplished what he wanted. He proved to the hordes that they could beat Roman main forces in the field. And he had acquired enough gold and plunder to convince any tribes who were still reluctant in their loyalties to give full support to their Hun overlords for fear they would be left out of the next campaign.

Now that Bleda was out of the way, Ch'ing began to plan his next step . . . an even larger campaign paid for with Roman gold. It took time to gather the men and wait for the right hour. The greatest delay came from the weather. A drought had dried up the grasslands and the horses of the horde were in poor shape. Most of the mares had miscarried, foaling prematurely due to the poor grazing and lack of water. Patience . . . patience. The time would come.

And it did. Rains finally came, turning the plains green with grass. The mares foaled on time. Then without warning, the Huns marched. Going farther east than in their first assault, they struck lower Scythia and Moesia, defeating the Roman Army on the Utus River, killing their commander, Arnegisclus, in a pitched battle in which the Huns suffered severe casualties. Their losses were made up in less than a week as reinforcements came in the thousands from the steppes.

Marcianopole was leveled and the Balkans stripped as they advanced into Greece where Attila stopped at the pass of Thermopylae.

Ch'ing tried to convince him to advance against the weaker Roman force, holding the pass, but he refused. Attila had dreamed that the pass would fall in on him, burying him under tons of stone. He would not move and nothing Ch'ing said could convince him to do otherwise.

Attila considered himself to be an intelligent man and it was not wise to go against the oracles of dreams. When he told them to Harmatta, the shaman had cast the bones and read the signs of the stars. Harmatta agreed with his master that the Huns must not enter the pass.

Ch'ing was royally pissed at the ignorant savages and as he made the sacrifice of two white doves to the spirits of his ancestors, he cursed them for being superstitious animals.

The Huns withdrew at the moment when the greatest cities of Greece were at their feet. Ch'ing had wanted them as a psychological blow to the minds of the Romans who still considered the Greeks to be the most cultured of all the races of man. The court in Constantinople even used Greek as their official speech.

CHAPTER FOUR

His escort had not been pleased at having to leave Rome and escort Casca the twenty-odd miles to Ostia, but he'd born it in as good a grace as he could. The smell of smoke drifted with them nearly the whole distance. It wasn't until they were less than five miles from their destination that the fresh air of the sea pushed back the remaining tinges of smoke and ash from the sky. Ostia was in a turmoil; evacuees from Rome and the surrounding countryside who still had money were trying to buy their way onto any ship that could float and was able to take them away from the mainland of Italia. Casca didn't give a damn which ship he was put on; any of them would serve just as well.

His reluctant companion had been of a like mind and took the first ship at the loading dock, a fat over-aged trader with a single mast that was already far overloaded with human cargo. Casca had everything he owned on his back and was a little surprised when the Gothic officer handed him a pack. From the feel and shape of it, Casca knew that Alaric had planned on his departure before their conversation on the walls. Inside were various items of weaponry including his sword and a set of barbarian armor consisting of a well-used breastplate and a simple cone-shaped helmet with a nose guard. Casca approved. The armor wasn't nearly as valuable as those of the praetorians, but where he was going, it would probably be wiser not to wear the colors and armor of Rome. This was the day of the barbarians and the world of Rome had shrunk severely.

The captain of the trader started to voice his protest at being forced to take aboard a passenger for no charge, but after the Gothic officer dangled him by his heels, head first, off the dock for a couple of minutes, the captain quickly became more reasonable. One thing about barbarians, Casca decided, was that they tended to settle arguments with as little bother as possible, believing in the direct approach to a problem.

Casca forced his way on board ignoring the captain's dirty, if soggy, glances. He really didn't care what anyone thought. He was drained emotionally. Rome was dying. He knew it had to come sometime but it was still a shock to witness the first enemy occupation of the Imperial City.

The captain of the trader was finishing the last of his haggling with the head of a family of merchants who now carried all they owned on their backs. In Rome they had left their fine home and gardens behind with all their furnishings. They were in abject terror of the rough hairy barbarians that stabled their horses in the Senate. Casca caught a look at the merchant's wife and daughter and thought the man had little to worry about as far as his women being molested by the savages.

It was shortly before midnight when the trader set oars to row past the tide and out onto the open waters. Casca picked a place near the stern and looked back. In the clear sky there was a glow on the eastern horizon. The fires in Rome were still burning. He felt a coldness in him that came not from the sea mist. It was a chilling of the spirit. If this were not the last chapter of Rome, he knew the final one could not be very far away.

He wished Vergix well and for the most part the same for Alaric and his dream, but he didn't think the world was ready for a joining of the two cultures just yet. Perhaps one day it would be. Then Alaric's hopes for a new vital civilization could become reality.

He was still in the same place when sunrise came—huddled in the stern, his cloak wrapped about his shoulders, squatting on a coiled length of hawser. The decks were packed to overflowing with people. He thought them fools. Where could most of them go? The world didn't belong to Rome any longer. Most of them would end up as slaves for the new masters. Even Spain was feeling the presence of the tribes who had moved over the Pyrenees into the warmer lands of Hibernia. There was nothing to stop them; perhaps there shouldn't be.

The captain started to approach his uninvited guest a couple of times to see if he couldn't get some form of payment from him, but changed his mind when the gray-blue eyes looked at him as if he were already a dead man. He left Casca alone. The slow wallowing tub made port at Messilia four days later and off-loaded its cargo of terrified humanity. Casca walked the gang-plank to dry land, leaving the refugees to their own devices. He stopped only to buy a few items he would need—a cooking pot of copper, a few strips of smoked meat and a spear. The merchants were driving the prices up, for since the influx of refugees, they were able to sell their wares for whatever they wished. Casca, however, paid them what he thought the items were worth, silencing any protest by touching the hilt of his sword. That combined with his barbarian dress was enough to put a halt to any objections.

Once his acquisitions were secured in his pack, he

left the walls of Messilia, not caring which road he took as long as it didn't lead to Rome. Here in southern Gaul the barbarian presence wasn't very evident. There were still some cities that had an uneasy truce with the tribesmen and Roman officials still administered the laws in their reduced domains.

The next few years found Casca's feet taking him from one country to another—Spain to Africa and back. It was easy to find employment; there were always those who had need of a strong sword to protect their goods. Empires might fall, but the business of commerce would always go on. The barbarians more so than the Romans had need of many items they couldn't make for themselves. Casca spent most of this time protecting those cargoes for a few coppers a day.

He was returning from a caravan trip to Hippo Regius when he heard Alaric had died of a sickness. He wondered what would become of Rome now. Alaric had become the shield of Rome. He had left most administrators in place to run the business of government. He even left the Romans an emperor in whose name he commanded what remained of the Roman legions. Alaric had been master of Italia but refused to claim the crown of the Caesars. Now that he was dead, who would take his place?

Casca decided that it didn't make any difference; what would be would be. He was tired of it all. He turned to the north toward the Rhine, heading against the flow of the migrating tribes. He was letting his instincts lead him even as he was ferried across the river barrier which had separated the barbarians from Roman Gaul for hundreds of years. He was going back to the northlands, drawn, as some birds unconsciously were, to take wing and return to some distant place to rest before it was time to fly again.

* * *

To any casual observer, he appeared to be no more than just another of the thousands of wanderers that were looking for work with their swords. The ragged furs and clothes he wore made it unlikely that any would try to rob him. He had nothing of value on him save some coins and his sword, and any who watched knew that the price of getting their hands on the blade would be more than the piece of steel was worth.

Casca's beard had grown full, covering his face; a robe of bearskin draped over his shoulders reached nearly to the knees. His tunic was almost worn out with age and wear. The blue dye had long since faded to washed-out spots of color that were lost under a coating of grime and sweat. He wore loose-fitting trousers, the legs of which were wrapped with bands of leather around his calves. His once fine Spanish leather boots had holes in them which he patched roughly with strips of boiled leather.

On his back was a round shield of hide with an iron boss in the center. Strung over his shoulder he carried a small bow of the style favored by the tribes of Scythia and a quiver full of iron-tipped hunting arrows. On his other shoulder he carried the remnants of the pack Alaric had given him. In his hand was a boar spear of fair steel, suitable for beast or man.

He was the same as any other mercenary. Though where he was now it would sometimes be days before he saw any sign of other human life.

The forests and plains had been drained of most of their people in the great migrations of the last twenty years. Entire tribes had left their native lands and crossed either the Rhine or the Elbe seeking warmer and richer lands to plunder and take for their own.

He spoke little when he did meet someone, and then it was only to get information about the lands ahead. He was going ever farther north. He wanted no part of the Empire and its new masters. The bitterness in his soul made his feet turn to the one place he had ever known peace.

Helsfjord waited for him. Helsfjord, where he had once been master and had buried the woman he loved. Perhaps his memory still lived there, though it had been so long ago that he was sure if his name did live, it was only as a distant half-believed legend. But it was the closest thing he had ever known to home, so there he would go.

On his trek there was no shortage of food to be had, for with the emptying of the lands, the animals had returned in strength. There were deer and bears in abundance along with smaller game which made it easy to keep his stomach filled, even if his mouth rarely tasted or cared what he put into it.

Finally he began to recognize landmarks and knew he was near. The first time he had come this way was with Glam, son of Halfdan the Ganger at his side. The memory was good. Then it had been in the dead of winter when they came to the edge of the mount and looked down on Helsfjord and the fort of Ragnar, whom he later killed.

Glam had been a giant of a man with a heart as big as his body and courage to match. The time they had spent together had been one of the few good memories he had known in his long years of wandering.

When next he hunted, he killed a deer and built a fire under an oak tree to burn part of the still-warm flesh as an offering to the shade of his long-dead friend.

The silence of the forests seemed to give him a sense of peace. The empty lands were what he needed. It gave him time to let his mind heal from the centuries of pain and slaughter. The leaves were just beginning to turn, adding a touch of red and gold to the green. The chill of the nights said it was time for the beasts of the woods to prepare for the long dark winter of the northlands.

With the turning of the leaves came also the mists which rose from the marshes and rich earth to swirl around one's feet and knees. In the morning it would rise to the tops of the trees so thick that a man could barely see his next step.

There were legends in many of the northlands that said it was foolhardy for one to venture out when the mists were on the earth, for something unspeakably evil lived in them.

Casca didn't believe the legends for he had been in the wet ground fogs many times, and the people of Helsfjord paid little attention to the legends either. But to the north of them, the barbarians, who would not hesitate to attack a force five times their number, would stay in their log houses when the fog came, keeping close to their fires.

He pushed the useless tale out of his thoughts and went on until he came at last to the same rise where he had first stood with Glam and looked down at the sheltered cove set in the rocks facing a stony beach.

There was Helsfjord. When he looked out to see the Hold, it was covered from his eyes by the morning sea fog which had come in with the tide. But he knew it was there and started the climb down. Anticipation and anxiety about what his welcome would be bothered him. Part of him wished to be remembered and welcomed, but he knew that he must let the past lie dead and just come to them as a wanderer seeking the rights of hospitality.

The silence came to him first, as he made out gray walls of native stone in the fog. At this hour there should have been the sounds of men and women going about their daily chores: forges being worked, the voices of children driving their cattle and sheep out to the fields.

There was nothing, only the rustle of the wind whispering over the stones. He moved his sword grip to a handier position. Slowly he approached the walls. He could just make out the gate as the fog was lifting, being burned off by the autumn sun.

Standing still, he waited, listening, watching as the fog rose ever higher, until the parapets on the ramparts were clearly visible. There was nothing. No hail from the walls to ask his name or business. No warriors on guard to protect those within its stone walls. Nothing but the silence of the wind. Unslinging his shield, he put it on his left arm, then moved carefully to the entrance, watching the slit-holes cut out for archers.

As he neared the gate, one of them swung open by itself, creaking heavily on hinges that needed oiling. There was a heaviness to the feeling that emanated from the Hold. It wasn't alive.

Before he entered, he knew there would be nothing for him at this place. It also had gone to the past along with everyone he had ever known or loved.

Inside the walls, the story was clear and its message an old one. The signs of fire were still on the walls where the wood buildings and storerooms had been put to the torch.

He wandered from room to room. The place had been picked clean. There was nothing left but broken pots and useless items that no one would bother to haul off.

Inside the hall where he had killed Ragnar were signs that a fight had taken place. Lying in the wreckage under a blanket of long-rotted straw was a broken sword. The metal of its blade had deep pits in it where the blood of its victim had eaten away at the iron, leaving the mark of the dead on it.

The first room he went to up the stairs was that of Lida, daughter of Ragnar and his own wife. This was where they had lived and loved. It had shared the same fate as the rest of the Hold; even the beds had been taken away for their new owners to sleep and love in.

There was nothing here save memories and ghosts, but at least some of the ghosts were ones he had loved. He would stay here alone until time's remorseless efforts forced him to leave.

Wandering through the dungeons and lower storerooms, he found a few things which would help him through the long coming winter. The raiders hadn't found everything. In one of the cells below, a door had been covered by a fallen beam concealing it from casual view. But he knew it was there, for this had been his home, and the room was near the cell where Ragnar had put him to starve to death.

In the room he found kegs of ale and beer and a couple of earthenware jugs with wine still in them. Also there were the things needed for daily life: lines and hooks for fishing, robes for warmth, and some odds and ends which he would need.

In one corner he found a small silver medallion that had been covered by a basket of woven reeds. Picking it up from the dust, he wiped off the face of it until he could make out what was on it . . . a serpent winding around the edge of the medallion encircling a jaguar in its coils.

He began to laugh; the sound startled him for a moment. It had been so long since a sound of that nature had come from his lips. The serpent and the jaguar. The Quetza and Teypeytal. Gods of the Teotec.

He had often wondered if Olaf Glamsson had made

it back home. The last he had seem of them were the red sails of their dragon ships disappearing over the horizon, as he tried to keep afloat after being washed overboard. But here he had evidence that they had made it back from the lands of smoking mountains and pyramids where priests and kings wore the feathers of rare birds and sacrificed the living hearts of men and women to their gods.

He chuckled in his isolation. *Gods*. He had been a god then, and now he too had returned to . . . what? Still chuckling, he hauled a keg of beer and one of the jugs of wine up to the hall and set them aside for later. First he would need to find food. Cursing himself for forgetting and having to make a second trip down into the dungeons for the fishing line and hooks, he went back for them and returned to the hall.

He found a chair in reasonable shape, set it back on its legs, and placed himself where he had sat before. At the head of the long table he and Lida had passed down judgments for their people. Their people. Perhaps there were still some who lived in the valley. . . . But he was tired; he would rest this day and on the morrow go to see if there were any left.

He spent that night in the chair wrapped in his furs. He didn't build a fire; it was too early for that. There might be some out there in the forests who would not welcome a stranger. He was stiff and his muscles ached when he pulled himself out of his slumber. He was thankful that no ghosts or memories had come to haunt his sleep.

He cleansed his mouth with a pull from one of the kegs of beer, then spat it out on the floor after rinsing off his gums to rid them of the night film. He fed on a piece of venison that was the last of his supply of food.

Gathering his weapons, leaving the rest of his gear behind, he went out of the Hold into the countryside where the valley had once been dotted with villages that had paid him fealty. There was no one there. Only empty ruins that time had not yet covered up.

It took him a couple of trips to haul back the grain and the few other items he had found in the deserted huts and houses. A brass pot, a bucket, some scraps of rope. Not much, but then he didn't need much. He was to be as alone as if he were a castaway on some far distant deserted island where no ships ever sailed.

The next weeks he spent gathering the food he would need for the long winter. The cove gave him fresh fish which he brought to the smokehouse to cure or hung in strips to dry. The forests provided venison and bear. Some of the meat he smoked, but when the nights became colder, he knew he could just leave the meat outside where the cold would keep it fresh for him.

The days grew shorter and the leaves fell from the trees, leaving them stark and bare to increasing winds that came in from the North Sea. He worked at gathering supplies, watching the skies turn ever darker until there were no more than three or four hours of true daylight before night fell.

The first lone chunks of ice started to drift with the tide into the cove as overhead flights of birds were heading south, some as far as Africa. The birds he looked for the most were the swans. Their wings gave strong graceful sweeps as they sailed through the skies.

Then came the quiet. The sounds of living creatures were gone. Those left were deep in their winter sleep. Those that could not sleep through the long dark would be the hunters, but he hadn't heard the cry of wolves yet.

For now he was alone with the creaking of the doors in the Hold or a low moaning when the sea wind found openings in the windows and halls. He took to walking the dark passages at night looking here and there—for what he didn't know. At times he would start to laugh for no apparent reason, as if he knew some great joke on himself.

The only room he fixed at all was the one he had shared with Lida, where he put a rough cot and a single chair to sit in by the fire. It would have taken too much effort to heat the great hall by himself and he didn't need it anyway. Lida's room was enough. There, in the dark, watching the fire flicker, tossing off small sparks to wink and fade, he felt close to her. Several times he caught himself just before he started to ask her something, then would remember she was long dead.

Time was slipping away from him, past and future. He began to find it difficult to tell which was the real *now*. Only once did he go to the grave of Lida at the field of Runes where they were wed and where he had destroyed the Saxon invaders. The spot where he had lain her body was gone. There was no way to tell exactly where the grave was; only the monolithic Rune stone with the writings of the Druids on it assured him that she was close by.

He stood by the Rune stone, the wind whipping his beard, sending small bits of frost to collect in the hairs, then melt under his breath. He saw her again as she was the day they wed. Hair of moonlight set with wild flowers of gold and blue, maidens singing as they shared the moment of joining and he kissed her sightless eyes.

He didn't notice the wetness that ran down his cheeks leaving a path through the grime and smoke until they were lost in his beard to turn into small frozen drops of loneliness. He seldom went near the field after that.

The winter storms began in earnest; gales of ice and snow changed the place into a magic frozen land of crystal palaces and ice orchards. He moved through the Hold, stopping now and then, cocking his head to the side as if someone had asked him something. Then he would snort and move on, making a small noise under his breath.

At times he would find himself sitting on the walls of the fort looking out at the cove which now was frozen over. He could hear the ice cracking under its own pressure as the ice forced against itself, expanding. It was in one of those moments he first heard the wolves in the distance.

He got to where he thought he recognized individual animals from their tones . . . the way they held a cry then wavered it on the end, letting the notes drift off to be lost in the cold night skies. If the mood hit him he would join them in their singing, raising his head, ignoring the crust of frost that gathered on him from the bitter sea mist. He would face the moon, imitating the wolves, and laugh in childish glee when one or more would answer him.

That winter wrapped itself about him; he no longer bothered to try and wash or shave off his ragged, hairy face. Even the scar on the side of his face running down to the corner of his mouth was partially lost in the hair and grime. His eyes sunk in, the gray-blue turning darker to the shade of pale coal. He cared nothing for the seasons, as winter slowly gave way to the spring. They were all the same to him. Another winter, then one more, until he lost track of them. Each day had a sameness to it that increasingly took his mind further away from reality.

Then came the winter of the freeze that split trees down the center. Even giant oaks ten feet around had their sap crystallize and expand until they burst open.

Casca hunted like an animal. When he saw seals on the ice, he wrapped himself in a fur robe, then would crawl out onto the ice. Twisting and turning he moved closer to them, imitating their movements, until he was close enough to make a cast with his spear. He seldom bothered to cook meat anymore; it took too much effort. And if the meat was fresh, he would sink his teeth into the still steaming carcass and tear off chunks of rich red flesh, half chew it, throw his head back and gulp it down the way bears or wolves do.

His hair had grown long enough to reach the small of his back and his beard hung in matted knots to his chest. His hands turned into claws. The nails, yellow, thick and curving, were talons with which he could tear meat from a kill and not have to use his knife. He had become half man, half beast. All those unfortunate enough to stumble upon him would surely think the creature before him was some kind of monster. And for that reason, no human being was safe in his presence, for Casca's mind was no longer his own.

Seasons turned one to the other. He gradually quit even trying to clean up the area he lived in. The Hold had been well on its way to becoming a cobweb; insect-, and rat-infested heap when he arrived, and by the end of the second year, that was exactly what it was.

The scraps of his meals lay about on the floors until rats hauled them off to their corners to feed on, until they learned that the strange animal that shared their home wasn't interested in them. Then they would just feed wherever they found food, even at his table while he was there. The more courageous of the pests would leap to the top of the table, give him a look of disdain, and drag a meaty bone off right under his nose.

The kegs of beer and wine Casca left alone, not wanting to drink what little remained of them, for then there would be no more. He just took a small cup once in a while to taste something besides water or bloody meat.

It was spring when company came to stay for a while.

Casca was sitting in his chair in the Great Hall nearly dozing when he heard a scratching sound near him. He sat still as he focused his eyes. A bitch wolf was standing in the open doorway. They watched each other— the yellow eyes of the wolf and the shadowed ones of the man. He saw that she was holding her front left paw off the floor, small drops of red dripping from it to the dust. Her sides were swollen, but her flanks were gaunt. She had been hurt and was obviously pregnant. He made no move as the wolf took one tentative step inside, then another and another, until she had crossed the hall and went into the dark space under the stairs that led upstairs to his room.

This was interesting. For the first time in longer than he could remember something had caught his interest. Why had the wolf come in here? Normally they avoided the Hold. True, when winter was at its hardest, some of them did come to the courtyard to take the scraps of his kills. Perhaps that was it. The bitch knew food was here. Probably she had hurt her paw and couldn't keep up with the pack, and from the way her sides heaved, he knew that her time for giving birth was not far off.

Rising from his chair, he took a couple of steps near the stairs, only to be met by a low warning growl. He backed off and went to his table. On it was a haunch of venison, fairly well chewed over, but there were still several large chunks of red meat on it. Picking it up, he tossed it under the stairs in front of the wolf. She made no move for the meat. Shaking his shaggy, dirty head, he went on up the stairs, leaving his new guest to her privacy.

Casca went out on the hunt. He found he was near the marsh following a deer trail. Stopping, he watched the wisps of vapor hover, float, rise and fall. Tendrils of mist reached out, then were whisked away to have their place taken by others.

Leaning up against a large rock, he saw it was the Rune stone and backed away from it. As he did he nearly stumbled when his foot bumped into a head-sized stone. He caught his balance, then nearly tripped over another. Looking down he saw the ground he was standing on was a depressed area about ten feet long and four wide. He had found Lida's grave. Slowly, he first knelt then lay down lengthwise on the grave, burying his face in the rich earth. He cried out for her as if his voice could bring her back to him, up from the pit in which she now lay for eternity.

Great wracking sobs tore at him until he could stand no more. Eyes blind, he rose and started to run, not knowing where. His legs had become leaden, not wanting to do his bidding. They were heavy, warm, wet things that pulled at him. He had run into the marsh. Pulling out of the mud pit, he fell down on a grassy hummock, chest heaving, mind torn. Sitting up, he ignored the slime that clung to him. It didn't matter. Nothing mattered. He just wanted to be left alone to forget. To get away from the pain of his existence and the terrible loneliness of his soul.

The mists moved in around him, touching him with fingers of damp air. He heard something. Tilting his head, he heard it again. Something familiar reaching out to him. The mists lightened then darkened, one then the other, blinking, turning one way then another, taking forms that meant nothing . . . yet something . . . that seemed to call to him from the shadows.

He heard his name . . . *Casca,* it came as a whisper over and over, *Caaascaa* . . .

A face danced in the ground fog, then another. Somehow he knew them all. It came to him that they

were the men he had killed. All around him they beck-
oned, many of them with the wounds he had given
them still on their faces.

Jubala, whom he had killed in the arena of Rome,
threw his head back and laughed, pointing at him, then
was replaced by Malgak, then Teypeytal, King of the
Olmecs. Faces rushed at him one after another, each
pushing the preceding one away. Jeering faces filled
with dead eyes of hate. Then they were all there.

Dozens of dead faces crowded around him, all pointing with accusing fingers. Goths and Vandals, Huns,
Saxons, Persians . . . faces he didn't even recognize,
but he knew it had been he who had given them their
deaths. . . . All mocked him with their dead eyes and
gaping mouths that spoke only in his memory where he
couldn't cut them out.

He screamed for them to go away, to leave him alone,
but their laughter just increased, building to a crescendo
of pain as they called for him to join them in death.

Tears ran down to his beard in rivers. He sobbed out,
"You know that I can't. I would if I was able but *He* won't
let me die, blame *Him,* not me. . . ."

They were gone, silence. Then another voice touched
him, one that he had laughed with in the past, one that
loved him well.

Glam was there, standing in the mists, a horn of mead
in his right hand, his great ax in the other. Throwing back
his head, he roared in laughter. "Don't let them get to
you, old friend. They're just jealous. If you hadn't done
them in then someone else would have. They all needed
killing and deserved what happened to them. They are
where they belong, each in his own special hell."

Glam drained his horn and threw it over his shoulder.
He put a large wispy hand toward Casca. "You have
friends waiting for you. Come to me. I have saved a place

for you by me in the Great Hall of Valhalla. Come to me, my friend . . ."

Casca repeated his earlier plea. "I can't. You know that. I would if it were possible."

Glam nodded his head, another horn appeared in his massive paw. He drained it in one draught, then wiped his walrus mustache with the back of his hand.

"There is another who is also waiting for you. She couldn't come but told me to tell you that she will wait for you. Lida said she will wait . . . a thousand years. . . ."

Glam began to fade. His voice a distant echo, he called to Casca, "A thousand years, old friend, a thousand years. Come to us when you can. . . ."

The mists whirled around faster and faster, taking his mind with it in a speeding whirlwind that had no beginning or end. It sucked him into it, drawing his soul out of him into the spirals of twisting vapor.

CHAPTER FIVE

When Casca came to, he was back at the Hold with no memory of how he got there. For the first time since he had returned, he felt lonely. The fort was an empty place, fit only for the dead, or lost memories, and his memory was back, crowding him.

He watched the skies, knowing his time here was growing short. He couldn't stay.

Two weeks later, he stood upon his walls wondering what fate had in store for him next. The wolf had departed that morning—with three new cubs; she had become strong, with Casca's help, and had given birth on the fourth day. Casca was almost sorry to see this little family leave; he was beginning to crave companionship for the first time in years.

Suddenly, a shadow in the brush by the base of the walls moved. His eyes clicked to it. It moved again. He dropped back behind one of the archer's slits to see but not be seen. Out of the brush a man staggered, holding his gut, weaving on weakened legs. He was obviously trying to reach the gate.

Casca ran down the stairs to the inner courtyard, then to the gate, which was locked from the inside. He put the side of his face to the thick wood and listened.

After a few moments, he heard the shuffling steps of the man outside. A weak pounding on the door followed by a young voice saying, "I ask for the rights of hospitality." Then a groan, a sliding sound, and silence.

Casca cautiously opened the gate a crack to peer out. His guest was lying face first in the dirt. Casca didn't know why he brought his visitor inside; the last guests here had not fared very well. Perhaps it was that the young man in his arms had claimed the ancient rights . . .

He carried the young man into the hall and laid him on a pile of straw. Then he brought water to wash away the crust of grime and blood on his guest's face; under it were the features of a fine-looking man of around twenty, fair-haired, good cleancut features, who had obviously had the crap beaten out of him. Not only that, but once Casca had removed the boy's hands from his gut, he saw that there was a deep stab wound in his abdomen. He had noticed the rest of the dark stains on the boy's tunic but just thought they were from the beating he had taken. On closer examination, Casca saw there were a number of other lesser cuts.

His guest had been in one hell of a fight, and it looked like he had come out second best. Well, he had seen men beat up before. But it was the stomach which concerned him. If the wound was not too deep, the youngster would have a chance to live. But if the stomach itself were punctured, then the boy would surely die.

He left him there and went out into the fields to find the things he would need. There was no great rush for the boy would either live or die, no matter what he did. While searching, he stopped to drink at a still pool and saw his reflection looking back.

He didn't recognize himself under the beard and hair or recall the last time he had seen his reflection in this same pond. It was a shock to see himself in this manner. He thought out loud, "If the stomach wound doesn't kill the boy, he will probably die of fright when he gets a good look at my face."

He returned to his foraging and returned to the hall where he put what he had gathered into a battered copper pot to boil. Then he set about scraping and hacking the growth of years from his face and head. It was a painful thing, for he had no razor and constantly had to rehone his knife, but still the blade tugged and pulled until his face felt more tender than the fanny of a newborn babe. At last he had most of it off, though there were still a few patches on his cheeks. His hair had been hacked off to a ragged shoulder level. By the time he had finished doing this, his pot was well aboil and the pungent aroma of herbs and wild onions filled the hall.

With a wet rag he wiped away the crust of blood from the youngster's stomach, exposing the cut. He then cleaned the boy's face and wet the youngster's lips. His guest came to, with a frightened look, but was calmed by being informed that he was being shown the rights of hospitality and had nothing to fear.

Casca raised him to a sitting position, his back against the wall, and went for the pot. Carrying it over to the pallet, he set it down and dug a wooden spoon out of the straw. With this he fed the boy his mixture of onions and herbs from a cup. Then he put his head down to the wound, pulled the edges apart and sniffed at the cut for a moment, then repeated the process again, making the youngster eat still more of the pungent mixture.

Again he pulled at the cut, opening it a bit more, and

put his nose down to sniff. Satisfied, he wiped off the cut again, sat back on his heels, and spoke to the boy who was looking at him as if he were mad.

Casca smiled so as not to frighten him too much. "No, I am not insane and I think you will live. If the blade had penetrated your stomach, I would have been able to smell the onions and herbs at the wound. There was no smell; therefore, you have a good chance to grow a full beard." The boy started to speak but Casca stopped him.

"There will be time for talk later; first I have to take care of your wound." Casca gathered some fresh cobwebs, of which there were plenty in the Hold, placed them around the cut after washing it again, then bandaged it as best he could with some of the cleaner strips of cloth available.

After finishing his medications, he told the boy, "Now you can talk, but there is no need if you do not wish to. You are welcome here."

"I am Rugisch," the boy began, "son of Torgau, sent to take the words for the tribes to send their leaders to a great gathering to form an alliance against the Huns."

Casca nodded in understanding. He always knew the day would come when the Huns would move farther west. The fact that they had come far enough that tribes from the North Sea regions were being asked to give aid surprised him.

Rugisch continued with his tale, "I was on my way to meet with the tribes west of the Danube when I lost my way. After many days of wandering, I was set upon by four men not too distant from this place. I killed one but was hit in the gut before I could make my escape. I have ridden one whole night and part of this day. My horse died under me this morning, just before I saw the walls of your fort."

Rugisch looked about the hall at the ruins and wreckage. "Are you the only one here, good sir?"

Casca asserted that it was so. Feeling no need to go into any extended explanations, he just said simply, "I found this place the way it is now and have spent some time here, for I had no need to go elsewhere and the isolation suited me well enough. That's all there is to my being here."

Rugisch accepted his host's explanation. Of course he had no other options if he wanted to keep breathing.

It was good for Casca having this young man there to take care of. It did much to return him fully to himself and the dreams had finally stopped coming to him. He was returning to reality though for a time he still felt as if he had been spiritually purged and drained.

He had been right about the wound—it stayed fresh with no sign of rot. Rugisch was up and moving about in two days, though slowly at first. But by the week's end, he had regained most of his strength and was ready to go on with his mission.

He spent some time trying to get Casca to go with him. Between the two of them, they would have a better chance of reaching all the tribes of the Rhine and Gaul. There was no longer any reason for Casca to remain in the Hold, so he agreed but said they would have to wait a few more days. He didn't want the wound to tear open and have to carry Rugisch a hundred or more miles.

Casca picked through the things he had brought with him when he had first arrived years ago, the weaponry given him by Alaric, and made them up a couple of packs. There were more than enough arms to go around.

In a corner of Lida's room, he found his helmet lying covered over by cobwebs and rusting. It took several hours of rubbing to remove most of the rust and restore it to a semblance of its former self.

By the time they set foot outside the walls for the first steps of their journey, Casca was his old self and looked the part, though he was still leaner than he had been. His eyes had lost their hot glow and faded back to their normal blue-gray.

This time when they climbed the ridge, Casca didn't look back. The past was dead. He still had uncounted tomorrows to contend with.

They made good time. The days were fair and the weather held no severe storms or early snow to hinder their steps. Of others they saw none, until they had traveled over a hundred miles and were near the river Maas. There they were ferried across by an old man who had stayed behind in the migrations because he was too old to make the march. He was glad to give them passage over the river in exchange for a haunch of venison. He was getting damned tired of eating fish and rodents.

He told Rugisch that the tribe he wanted to find had left their lands and had gone in the wake of the Franks across the Rhine into Gaul. It was there he must go if he wished to see them.

Rugisch was dejected by this news. If his kinsmen had crossed the Rhine, then they would not be likely to offer any help, if it meant a march of several hundred miles to do so. But still he had been instructed to deliver his father's message and would do so no matter what the difficulties or response.

Gradually, as they neared the Rhine, they came upon increasing signs of human habitation. A farm, some plowed fields, cattle grazing; from these they obtained directions and went on their way. Casca had a few coins in his purse that he had saved along with his weapons. These served to keep them fed once they reached lands where they could buy food.

Rugisch had some small bars of silver of his own, and between them they had no problem in getting the things they needed most, which consisted of two horses—a pair of over-aged geldings. But they went much faster now that they would set foot on well-used trails and eventually the roads of Rome.

They passed through several well-populated villages and then were over the Rhine and into Gaul proper. From there it was easy going. The new masters of Gaul seemed to Casca not much different than the previous masters there. The land looked the same and the fields were well-tended, ready for harvest. It appeared the rough tribes of Germania had been gentled somewhat by easy living and fair weather.

They were left alone and were not delayed on the roads by other than normal questioning looks from those they passed. Casca was surprised to see several patrols of Roman cavalry on the roads. When he had last been through here, all was controlled by Visigoths or Franks. Now he saw in the faces of the legionnaires about an equal number of Italian and Germanic faces. Alaric was long dead. The Empire had returned, a bit feebler, but still master in name if not in fact.

At Lugdenesis they found the Suevii and their leader, one Svatova, an uncle by blood on Rugisch's mother's side, serving with the federati, assigned to the local garrison under the command of a praetor.

They entered the wall of the city and found quarters among the cousins of his tribe in their barracks. His uncle provided the light cavalry for the region, who were respected allies of the Romans who were very short of horsemen themselves, and had to rely on their new associates to provide them.

They welcomed Rugisch as a kinsman and Casca because he was with him. Casca stayed to himself. He still felt awkward with so many people around him and left Rugisch to meet his uncle alone.

When Rugisch returned, it was as expected. His uncle could do them no good. He had a contract with the Romans and it couldn't be broken at this time. Yes, he knew the Huns were on the march and many cities had fallen to them. But there was nothing he could do about it. They were not his lands anymore. Where he was now was what concerned him, and the Huns would never get this far. . . . There was too much between them for him to be concerned about the savages of the steppes. He had problems enough now with countering raiding bands of outlaws or renegade tribesmen who preyed on unwary travelers or convoys of food destined for the Roman garrisons.

He offered Rugisch a position in his cavalry and said there would be a place for his strange friend if he wanted it. Rugisch turned down the offer on his part but relayed the rest of the message to Casca who said he would think about it for a time before giving his response.

Casca thought about it for some time, then decided to pass on the offer. Rugisch asked him if he would prefer to stay with him for a time and return with him to meet his father, who should be on the other side of the Tsai River.

For Casca one place was as good as another. He could feel the storms of war gathering, so what difference did it make where he was. There would always be work for one such as he.

The Empire had been in a state of confusion ever since Alaric had sacked the city. It had been unable to regain its full power. Much of the spirit of the Roman citizens was broken as a result.

His young companion was well-educated on the events of the times and what was taking place where. His father had sent him to schools in Rome and Constantinople to learn the ways of those he would have to deal with in the future. He kept up a running dialogue, bringing Casca up to date on all that had transpired since he had crossed the Rhine and gone to Helsfjord.

Honorius had died and his nephew, Theodosius, was for a time master of both the Western and Eastern Empires. However, Galla Placidia, the sister of Honorius, had her son Valentinian lay claim as the legitimate heir of Honorius and appealed to Theodosius in Constantinople to acknowledge their claim.

Theodosius was reluctant to give up his claim to the Western throne, but he had troubles enough in the East without having to deal with intrigues elsewhere.

Since the death of Honorius, the court at Ravenna was anxious to keep their independence from Constantinople and elected one of their number as the new Emperor of the West. Theodosius decided to honor Placidia's claim when she showed him she had the support of Bonifatius, the Roman commander in North Africa. Bonifatius had it in his power to stop most of the grain shipments to Italy and a good portion of the produce also went to feed the throngs of the Eastern Empire. This in itself could cause more trouble than Italy was worth, for the East would have to pay for the misery that starvation and pestilence would bring.

He granted Placidia's demands. Valentinian was proclaimed Emperor of the West. Theodosius then sent troops to take back power from Johannes the Usurper. Ravenna was taken through trickery with little trouble and Johannes had his head removed from his body as an example to all who lay claim to the royal purple without the consent of the East.

The matter in Rome had to be settled quickly for there were new evidences of the expansionist designs of the Huns. This was no time for Rome to fight against herself. Rome had to rely on hiring many barbarians to defend her, even to using Huns themselves as light cavalry, and its problems with the Church were nearly as bad as the political situation, with different factions fighting among themselves, each crying out that others were false in their beliefs concerning the divine nature of God and his relationship with Jesus.

But now the greatest danger was not in the provinces that had been lost, but in the new threat from the East.

There were intrigues upon intrigues. Gaiseric the Vandal had decided that the new alliance between the Suevii and Visigoths of Spain and Gaul were a threat to his African Empire. So he made overtures to the King of the Huns, trying to persuade him to attack his enemies on the continent, hoping he would be in a position to pick up the pieces after both sides had exhausted themselves in battle.

The Emperor Valentinian had problems at home with his sister, Honoria. He had arranged for her to marry a prominent senator but she, as was the way of women, decided not to follow his wishes. And just to piss him off, Honoria offered her hand in marriage to Attila.

This, of course, was not meant seriously. But Attila used the offer as a pretext to make demands on

Valentinian, demanding that he be sent his bride, and as her dowry—half of the Western Empire.

Casca took all this in with a deepening sense of irony. For all of the blood and passion, it didn't make much difference. Things were always the same: someone was always trying to screw up someone else.

As it turned out, they didn't have to travel all the way to the Tsai River; instead, they met the first elements of Rugisch's tribe heading west between the Danube and Aquincum.

Rugisch called to the first outriders and identified himself. He and Casca were immediately taken to his father, who was at the head of their tribe. To the rear, in a line that stretched for miles, a nation was on the move. Everything they owned was packed on the backs of horses or being hauled in large, two- and four-wheeled wagons.

Rugisch's tribe wasn't the only one on the move. There were Goths, Vandals, Romans and the people of a dozen races—refugees from the hordes that were sweeping all before them. The Huns had broken out and were heading west.

Rugisch's father, Torgau, greeted his son emotionally from horseback, gripping his boy's right arm with his own withered right hand. He was barely able to keep his dignity in front of his warriors.

He was a rough-looking old pirate. One eye—the left—was gone; a scar creased his brow to his cheek on the left side. He wore a good tunic of blue linen and carried a copy of a Roman shield of the oblong style on his back. He was about the same height as Casca but thicker in the body and chest. He was an old warhorse, but from the looks of him, one who could still put up a hell of a fight if pushed, and he was being pushed.

That they had fought hard was evidenced by the

number of wounded they carried with them in their wagons. They also had a number of Hunnish prisoners. All the captives were nobles of either the Huns or one of their allied tribes. They were kept alive so that Torgau could eventually exchange them for members of his own tribe who had fallen into the hands of the Huns.

While Rugisch and his father talked, Casca rode back to get a look at the prisoners. The last time he had seen Huns was on the borders of China where they were known as the Hsiung-nu. That had been years ago.

From a distance, they appeared to be the same, but on closer examination, he saw that many of them had features of the West mixed with the flat faces and high prominent cheekbones of the steppes. There had been much intermingling of bloodlines since last he had fought against them; several even had eyes the same color as his.

But, if they had some of the blood of the West in their veins, it had not diluted their primal savagery; in that they were the same. Among the prisoners were several who had no blood of the East in them. They were the allies of the Huns and rode with them willingly for the sake of plunder or revenge.

Under his gaze, they were impassive as they stumbled along on feet that weren't used to walking. The guards kept them chained together and under constant watch. Any who looked as though he were even thinking of giving them trouble was immediately impaled on the point of a spear.

When Casca returned to Rugisch, he and his father had pulled off to the side letting the column pass them as they talked. He welcomed Casca with even more interest and a degree of affection since Rugisch had told him of Casca's saving his life. There had been two other sons, but they had lost their lives in battle on the banks of the Tsai trying to prevent a crossing by Huns.

Casca stayed with the column for another three days before deciding to head out on his own. He still wasn't used to having so many people around him. There were just too many; he couldn't sleep with the noise of riders and wagons going by. Besides, he wasn't sure if Rugisch and his father could deal with the Huns if they caught up to them. He didn't feel like getting involved in a losing battle right at the start. They were good warriors with plenty of courage normally, but they had had the crap kicked out of them and were still too demoralized to be an effective force. It would be some time before they regained their confidence.

After informing Rugisch of his decision to take off, he was given a message by his father to take to the Roman commander of Gaul. Perhaps now they would give them aid, for if the Hun was not stopped soon, they would reach the sea.

Turning his horse back the way he had come, he left the slow-moving line of refugees behind him. It felt good to be alone again.

The return trip gave him time to think about the Huns. They were not acting in the same manner as when he had fought them before. Their basic battle tactics hadn't changed much, but now they were using pressure in a different manner than they had in the Far East. Now they would threaten here and then strike somewhere else, leaving enough men behind to tie up forces that could have been used against them at their real target. From what he had learned from Torgau about the new Hunnish methodology, someone was giving them some pretty damned sophisticated advice and they were taking it. They no longer blindly charged, simply trying to smash an opponent under the hooves of their war-horses.

Sometimes they still used the old trick of faking a retreat to suck their prey in until he was over-extended, then turn when the pursuer had exhausted himself, break them up into small units and dispatch them one at a time at their leisure. Now they timed things carefully. The rate of march of their enemies and place of battle were nearly always of their choice.

They would hit an enemy column and whiplash it by striking at the head, forcing the rear to rush to give assistance, then withdraw. Once the enemy column was stretched out again, they would repeat the attack, this time hitting the rear elements, forcing the leading units of the column to rush back to the rear. After this had been done a few times, the enemy was so tired, demoralized, and exhausted they were easy to deal with.

At Vindonissa, he was stopped by a patrol of mounted federati, Frankish cavalry patrolling the river banks of the Upper Rhine to the Alps.

They had heard the Huns were moving but thought he was overreacting to the threat. If the bowlegged little bastards ever did show their pushed-in faces on their side of the river, they, the greatest warriors in the world, would teach them what it meant to fight real men.

Casca had heard that kind of crap more than once and knew there was no sense in trying to tell them any different. They would just have to learn the hard way.

He rode with them for a piece, then went on his own once more. He did find out who was commanding the Roman forces in the West—Flavius Aetius. That was who he would try to see. Perhaps he would listen from what the Franks had told him. Aetius was a good leader who had fought the Huns before.

CHAPTER SIX

Aetius had long been the man most familiar with Huns of any leader in Rome. More than once he had been sent to live with them as part of a hostage exchange. He had known Attila when they were both young men and taken some pleasure in always being able to get the better of him in every deal they had made, whether it was trading horses or gambling. He had always taken an air of superiority around him as he felt he represented the culture of Roman civilization.

Attila had to work hard to control his temper when Aetius used to needle him about taking up the marathon run for his tribe. He had even put him down in their wrestling matches using the tricks taught him by his Greek tutors. The only thing that Attila could do better was to ride and shoot at moving targets from horseback while at a full gallop. Aetius denigrated these accomplishments as being only natural for one who had the intelligence and smell of a horse.

Attila swore in his heart that one day he would make the smug superior Roman eat his words, showing him once and for all who was the better.

After Aetius had reached his maturity and gained rank in the legions, he had often gone to the Hun encampment to talk with old Kara-ton or Attila's uncle Ruga about hiring a few thousand of his warriors to fight for him as light cavalry and would always end up paying less than half of what it would have taken to get Vandals or Goths to fight for him. Even then he would pay in gold which was less than pure.

He knew the Hun better than anyone else did, and though he had been in and out of favor at the court several times and lost his office more than once, he was the one they always sent for when they needed the horsemen of the Huns to perform some chore that no one else would take.

He understood their way of thinking and knew that it was both their strength and their weakness. The Huns could be beaten, but it wouldn't be easy.

Aetius was pleased at how things had finally come his way. He was now the *magister ultriusque militiae,* the supreme commander of Roman forces since his predecessor, Felix, had been assassinated.

He was the real power in the West now, but still he had to deal with the Senate and the Emperor. Because of the distance they kept from the field, they were constantly able to interfere with his plans. It was a temptation to let Attila take all of Italy and liquidate the smug officials. Then he would drive the Huns back and make himself Emperor. But that, he sighed, didn't look to be very likely. He was a soldier and couldn't let his country be overrun and put to the sword.

And he had other things to do now. Attila was coming. They both knew that one day they would meet on the field of battle. There could be no other way, it was their fate.

Casca was admitted to the presence of Flavius Aetius.

The two men eyed each other. Casca liked the look of the Roman *magister*. He reminded him of some he had met when Rome had consistently produced great leaders. It was good to know there was at least one left.

Aetius was around fifty but moved with quick, sure actions. His eyes were clear and he had an intensity to him that spoke of his years of command.

Aetius listened to the message from Torgau. He had met the old man several times and knew that he was a solid thinker not given to flights of imagination; in fact, Torgau didn't have any imagination.

As Casca spoke, Aetius gave careful attention to the message but still kept an eye on his guest. He was a tough-looking brute who appeared to be a barbarian but spoke the tongue of Italia as only one born to it can.

Casca finished his report still at attention.

Aetius cocked an eyebrow. "Your name, man?"

Casca gave the Roman salute, striking his chest with his right first and replied in military fashion: "Sir, I am Casca Rufio Longinus."

Aetius looked at him carefully. "You're a Roman?"

"Aye, Domini."

Aetius leaned back in his chair, pleased that he had been right in his suspicions about the man in front of him. The brute was not only a Roman but had also served in the legion; it was written all over him.

The fact he was dressed as a barbarian didn't surprise him; there had been many in the last few years that had gone over for one reason or another to live with the tribesmen.

He thought about the message from Torgau. It confirmed much of what he suspected. That was the reason he was here at this place at this time. He was waiting for Attila to come to him.

"Sit down." He indicated the other chair. "Casca Longinus, wasn't it?"

Casca did as he was asked, pulling the chair up closer to the desk, glad to be off his feet.

Aetius watched his face. "Have you fought the Hun before?"

Casca thought about how best to answer him and decided to speak in generalities. "Yes, many times in one place or another."

Food and drink were brought in. Aetius poured wine for Casca and spring water for himself. He was not one to drink when talking business. As Casca had no business of any kind at the moment to bother him, he drained his cup.

Aetius gave him another once-over. "Do you know," he continued, "what the message you have just given me means?"

Casca looked him straight in the eye. "Yes, and if I were you, I think I would believe it. The Huns are coming. Even now they should be close to crossing the Danube. There won't be much time before they're sitting on your doorstep."

Aetius called for his orderly to bring more wine. They spent several hours together that night talking by the light of the oil lamps, each feeling out the other. They found they had much in common in their knowledge of the Huns and of warfare.

When pressed by Aetius as to more information about his past, Casca gave him no dates, saying only that he had first encountered the Huns while in service of the Emperor of China some years before.

Aetius was fascinated. He had never met one of his own race that had been that far before. He had talked once with a merchant from Kushan that had been all the way on the Silk Road. But the man knew only the prices of goods and slaves, nothing of the manner of warfare waged by the different lands he passed through.

Aetius found his scar-faced guest a wealth of data; the man had amazing recall. Soon they were involved with arguments over the way one situation or the other should have been handled.

Casca told of the manner in which the Huns of the Far East had been beaten by the armies of Emperor Tzin and before that by other generals of China. That gave Aetius some encouragement.

By the time Casca had left to sleep in a tent provided by his host, he knew that Aetius was the hope of Rome, the only one who could beat Attila if he were given the means to fight properly.

Aetius watched the broad back of Casca disappear from sight as the flap of his tent was closed behind him. He knew he wanted him, no matter where he had come from or how much he tried to keep his past a secret. He knew how to judge character and this one would be very valuable to him.

This man, Casca Longinus, had a strange quality to him. Even when he spoke of battles long past, such as those that took place at Cestiphon over a hundred years ago, he gave one the impression that he had been there, that he had seen the things he spoke of as history with his own eyes.

Aetius pushed his cup of water away, replacing it with one of wine now that he was alone. The man was an extraordinary storyteller. Aetius almost wished the Romans still used chariots. He could see a use for the tactic Casca had told him of, where chains were stretched between the chariots and used to knock the legs out from under the horses of the attacking Hsuing-nu. That showed some original thinking. He liked a man who used his mind as well as the sword. Swords could always be bought with gold but a man who thought was too valuable a commodity to be let go easily.

Aetius thought long that night. He didn't have much time. He hadn't told Casca that he had already had several reports in, sent to him by fast riders. The Hun was closer than he knew and the tribe of Rugisch and Torgau was no more.

Calling for his secretary, he wrote letters which were sent out at first light, letters to the Visigoths and the Burgundians, to the Salian Franks and others of the Germanic tribes. He had fought against all of them at one time or another, but now they had a greater enemy coming to them. He had to convince them that for now they would have to put their differences aside and fight together or they would all be destroyed separately.

He needed their cavalry and slingers, their archers and spearmen. Most of all, he needed their courage in battle. He knew that there was no way for him to muster enough forces to face Attila alone. If he stripped Italy of men and brought them to Gaul leaving Rome defenseless, then Attila would simply turn and head straight for Rome.

The Hun had the ability to take advantage of any situation and react to it faster than their opponents. By the time Aetius could turn his men around and take them back to the defense of Italy, the damage done might be too great for him to have any hope of driving the Huns out.

At their rate of march, they could be across the Rhine in two weeks. It would take him at least two months before he would be ready to counterattack. He knew that someone was going to have to pay the price for that time.

Aetius was anxious, troubled. He had far too few

men to have any real chance of victory in the morning, but there was no other choice. They had to fight and fight now. He gave thanks that Theodoric, King of the Visigoths, had decided to come to his side.

Theodoric's messengers had finally come to him with the word that, in this case, their interests were the same as the Romans', for if Orleans fell, there would be nothing to stop Attila from reaching the coast or even Spain.

The Visigoths would fight now rather than when they would have to stand alone, their backs to the sea. If they were to survive, they had to help and do it now.

Theodoric himself had appeared two days earlier in the vanguard of his army. Among them were many tough old warriors and veterans, many of whom had been at the sack of Rome under Alaric. Theodoric had sent out the call to arms and none that could ride or hold a spear would be permitted to remain behind. This was the final stroke; they would either win this time or Europe would fall to the Huns.

Aetius sent for his new centurion. Casca showed up in a few minutes wearing his new armor, a gift from Aetius and with the insignia of his rank. He, like Aetius, had been poring over the plans for the morrow. He sat across from his commander on a wooden stool.

"Casca, can you think of anything else we might do this night, or anything we have overlooked?"

Casca removed his plumed helmet with the red horsetail brush, setting it beside his stool. "No, I can think of nothing else now. If we wait for the right moment, we will have a chance. Attila has been in the field too long and his army has stripped the land for leagues around. There is nothing left for them to feed either themselves or their horses on. They are tired and that is what we must use against them. This is the first time they have made the mistake of keeping the same force in constant engagements for two continuous seasons. Attila has broken the rules and if fortune smiles on us, he will pay for it."

Aetius wiped his forehead with the back of his hand. It was hot even for July. "I hope so. If your plan works, I'll raise you to the rank of praetor myself, with or without the approval of the Senate or Valentinian. Now go and get some rest. We both will have to be moving out in a few hours."

Casca saluted, striking his right hand across his chest, and picked up his helmet, leaving Aetius to his plans. He knew the Roman general would rest this night and there was still a distance to go before they reached the fields of Mauriacus.

Casca was restless, too; the heat of the evening was oppressive, making the air thick and hard to breathe. Instead of going to his cot, he walked through the encampment, passing between the different units which were grouped according to their race and tribes. He acknowledged the hailings from the sentries and kept on going, passing the odd mixtures that the future of western civilization depended on.

Burgundians, Salian Franks and the Visigoths made up the largest number of barbarians who would fight under the eagles of Rome the next day. There were several units from half a dozen other tribes who were put into one single regiment under the leadership of a Briton warchief, who had the marks of the Pict on his face, blue whorls tattooed on his cheeks and patterns of mystic design on his chest and arms. A strange force.

The Romans supplied most of the infantry. It was they who would be the anvil against which the Hun must strike. If they held, then the cavalry of their Germanic federati would do the rest.

He returned to his own tent to sit before the campfire watching the coals glow and hiss. Even in the warmth of summer, there was something about a fire at night that made things seem better; it gave one a feeling of security.

The scar running from his eye to his cheek tingled, prickly from the heat of the campfire. *Once more I fight for Rome.*

Grunting, he rose to enter his tent, closing the flap behind him. He had things yet to do this night. When he came out of his tent, it was as a barbarian. His Roman armor was in a sack in his hand. Under a thin tunic of well-worn cloth, he wore a jacket of chain mail. He looked the part of barbarian right down to the thongs of his leggings. He tied his bundle to the back of his saddle and mounted the horse he had selected.

The horse was one of the tough, ugly, foul-tempered Hun war ponies, a hooked-nose beast that could live on gravel for a week. Casca still had a bruise the size of a dinner plate on his right thigh where the bastard had tried to make a eunuch of him.

If things went right, he would be on the walls of Orleans in the morning. It was his job to give the defenders their orders. Those in the city were waiting for him. Three days earlier, Visigoths, dressed in the same manner as he was now, joined in with an assault band of Huns going against the walls. They shot several arrows over the walls with the message that on this morning at first light, Casca would be coming to them. They were to have the gate ready to open at a moment's notice. They had signaled their assent at the hour when Venus appears in the night sky by lighting three fires on their parapets. They let the fires burn for five minutes, then extinguished them. They would be ready.

A troop of Roman cavalry arrived to provide Casca with an escort through their lines. If any of their men saw him in this dress, he would have his ass filled with missiles of many designs before he could protest.

Once through their outposts, he was on his own. He kicked his beast into a reluctant trot and headed into a grove of trees. He had about a four-hour ride before he would be able to see the walls of Orleans.

At dawn when the Huns made their regular morning attack, he had to be there. He rode hunched over through the trees and brush, keeping his head down to avoid the whipping branches that tried to stab his eyes out. Once he was out of the trees, the going was easier and he had a clear run to Orleans.

He swore that his horse was intentionally running at a stiff-legged gait just to fracture his spine and ruin his butt. Casca was positive that because he had spent so many weeks in the saddle that he could clinch the cheeks of his ass together and be able to crack walnuts. Gods! How he hated horses!

The acrid smell of wood smoke from a thousand camp-fires reached him before he even came within eyeshot of the city. When he did see it, he was on the edge of the cleared area, which had once been farmland, leading all the way to the walls.

He eased the pony into a walk, not wanting to attract any attention. He passed a couple of patrols and waved at them in a comradely fashion, not stopping. The day was beginning to break as he came to a small knoll and pulled up. From there the gates of the city were clearly seen; there was little more than a mile to go.

The light of the new sun was turning the skies red over the fields. The sounds of the Hunnish encampment reached out to him . . . that peculiar distant murmur of thousands of men being formed up into ranks.

Over to the west he could make out several large devices. Obviously siege-machines had been built during the siege and were nearly ready to be put into operation. A mixed detachment of Huns and Gepid cavalry formed up right below him. That was good. He looked the enemy warriors over. They weren't in too good a condition and neither were their animals. Attila had to take the city soon or his men would begin to starve. It was too bad they couldn't eat the gold and silver in their wagons.

He did recall a time when he had seen a man ordered to dine on such a meal. It had been at the court of the Sassinid King Shapur II, who had ordered a thief's mouth filled with molten gold. The idea of it made his teeth ache.

Horns were sounding; skin-topped drums picked up the beat. It would be soon. Taking his shield from the straps where it hung on the other side of the pony, he put it on his left arm. The shield would be his key to getting inside the gates.

On the outside of the shield was the emblem of a gold eagle flying. When that was spotted, the gates would open for just enough time to let him enter. If he was too slow or the Huns too close, he knew they would be shut in his face.

The Huns and Gepids moved forward, staying just out of bow range. He did the same, careful to draw no attention to himself. To his left he saw about five hundred men. They looked like Alans carrying scaling ladders toward the walls. Casca moved in among the horsemen mingling with the mass as they started to ride at the walls, drawing their bows back.

Casca kicked his horse to the front of them, then broke away heading straight for the gates, his shield raised high showing the emblem of the gold eagle. It also gave him a little protection in case someone on the wall hadn't gotten the word and tried to nail him. Several did let loose shafts; they were not near to hitting him but it made it look good.

It was easier than he had thought it would be. He pulled the slip knot on his pack, grabbed it and hit the ground running, letting his horse go back to its original owners with his curses. He had to dismount because the gate he was using was too small for a horse to get through. The door swung open and he was inside before the Huns outside had a chance to figure out what had happened.

CHAPTER SEVEN

Immediately he was taken to the headquarters of the *praetor militarium,* where he had his staff gathered, waiting for Casca's report and orders. The praetor, Commitus, was showing the effects of the siege. Fifty was too old for all this. He hadn't had a full night's sleep in weeks. The tension left him with a semipermanent nervous tic at the corner of his mouth.

Casca saluted as Commitus rose to greet him and receive what he hoped would be more than a message— a salvation. Casca sat at the head of the table where he could see the faces of all the officers present and made his report.

They listened without interruption until he informed them of the situation and what role they were to play. The last part didn't sit very well with them, but Casca left them few alternatives in the matter. It was a case of do as they were ordered in the coming battle and maybe get killed, or not do it and be killed for certain.

There was no way they had a chance to win unless they obeyed. That argument stopped their objections. They were to be ready to move at an instant's notice with all the manpower they had, including any civilians that hadn't already been pressed into service.

Casca changed back into his Roman uniform and armor, complete with his badges of rank, and went to the walls to observe the enemy.

The Huns weren't seriously attacking. They were just keeping those inside nervous and doing a damned fine job of it. When the siege machines were ready, the main assault would come. Once they reached the walls—with the battering rams and three-story mobile troop platforms from which they would be able to attack the walls by just running over a ramp—it would mean the death of the city.

From what Aetius had learned from the prisoners, the machines would be ready in just two more days. Therefore, the conclusion of the siege had to be reached before they could be used.

Standing on the walls, he saw a strong party of Huns escorting two men. They came under flag of truce to parley. Commitus joined Casca on the wall. He gave the order for his men to stop their fire and let the party approach.

They halted just out of bow range. Their leader called out to those on the walls: "I am Ongesh, servant to Attila. I bring you the master's words, heed them and live. If you this day open your gates to us, he will spare your lives and your city. What good is the wealth of your city if you are dead? Submit and live. There are no other choices. My master makes this offer only once to show his mercy. He wishes to avoid further bloodshed. You have fought well and bravely. There will be no dishonor in surrendering to our forces which outnumber you by at least ten to one." He paused for effect. "You have until the sun reaches its zenith to make your reply. After that, there will be no further communication." He pointed back to the rear where one of the siege machines was being pulled up by captives, straining to haul the several tons of the battering ram as their backs were laid open by Hun overseers.

"There will be more machines tomorrow, enough to breech your walls with ease. These are the words of Attila. Think over what I have said. Your hours are numbered."

When they rode away, Casca noticed the figure of a slightly built man in the rear of the party looking as if the armor he was wearing wasn't natural to him. He had a look to him that was definitely not Germanic or Hunnish.

Commitus joined Casca. "What do you think of the offer?"

Casca grinned evilly. "You think the Huns will honor his pledge if you surrender to him? I think not and to prevent the world from knowing he lied, I'll give you odds that the only one in that party that spoke our tongue was the leader. Anyway, in order to keep the world from finding out he's a liar, he will have to kill everyone here and he will. Don't even think about surrendering or I'll kill you myself before the first Hun enters the gates."

Commitus was not a complete coward, but the manner in which his guest spoke left no doubt in his mind that if he made any attempt to parley, he would most certainly die. There was no profit in that and Commitus was a practical man. The odds were better with the centurion's offer; at least that way he had a chance to live.

Casca didn't trust the praetor. He moved to a spot on the wall where he could protect his back from Commitus in case he got the idea that it would be better to eliminate him and make a separate deal with Attila. On his way he picked up a pilum from a weapons rack. There was nothing to do except wait until midday when they would return for their answer.

The other soldiers on the wall kept their distance from him. He had a look to him that said it was better to leave this one alone.

As promised, the Huns returned to get their answer. The same man, Ongesh, led them. The Huns stood still in their saddles as Ongesh called out to the walls. "What is it to be? Life or death? I await your answer."

Casca gave him his answer in a manner which would insure there would be no further parley. Raising up to stand on the crenelated parapet, he took a deep breath, drew back, and then, with all the strength of his body, hurled the weighted pilum up in a long arcing throw. The spear entered the ribcage of Ongesh's horse, nearly hitting Attila's minister in the leg. The horse went down screaming, blood frothing from its nostrils. It was lung shot. Ongesh threw himself from the saddle to avoid being rolled on. He stumbled to his feet in a rage.

Casca called down to him: "You look better that way. Toads should not ride horseback and from the look of your legs, you could probably hop faster than your horse could run."

Ongesh nearly had a stroke; blood rushed to his head, nearly making him fall back down. He screamed in rage; he wanted to get his hands on the Roman on the wall who dared break a truce and mock him. Naturally, Ongesh didn't recall the times he had had messengers killed for just bringing bad news, but that was an entirely different matter.

One of his riders rode to him, dismounted, and gave Ongesh his horse. He swung up in the saddle, leaving the warrior whose horse he had taken to hang onto the tail of another's animal, and run back to their lines with awkward bandy-legged leaps as he hung onto the tail.

Ongesh stopped when he was sure he was out of range. That had been the longest spear cast he had ever seen. He could hear the man on the wall laughing at him. "Go ahead, laugh now," he screamed. "On the morrow, I will have your head for this. You will die, all of you, and your women will carry the seed of our warriors in their bellies. Your children shall be slaves for as long as they live and used as such. All males will be castrated. You will pay for this. I swear it upon the head of my father." Raising up in his saddle, he pointed his finger at Casca. "And you, I will take myself. You will beg for the mercy of death." Whipping his horse around, he rode back to inform Attila of the city's response to his offer.

Ch'ing was sulking in his tent. Attila would not listen. His advisers and warchiefs had convinced him to go into Gaul. Ch'ing Li had time and again advised against such an action. He did not want to have to fight on more than one front. It was not the time to conduct another major campaign.

They had been in the field for too long. Their men needed rest, time to recuperate and train replacements. If they waited until the next spring, they would be able to take Italy. It would give them time to negotiate treaties with the Visigoths and the Franks, which would provide them with a passive buffer to the west. If they husbanded their strength at this time, they would have the power to conduct the war in Italy and keep the Eastern Empire out of it by making alliances with the White Huns in Kushan and even the Persians. Just the threat of such an alliance would prevent the Eastern Emperor, Marcian, from being able to lend any effective support to the Western Empire. Fools!

History had proven that Constantinople would always put their interests before that of Rome. Savages! They would not listen and learn. Attila was determined to have everything at once. He agreed they did not have the resources to attack Rome this season, but there was always Gaul.

Ch'ing Li knew the price would be great. He had no

doubt they could take the city, but they would have to pay for it later. Sighing regretfully, he sent for his masseur to rub away the tensions of the day. There was one saving factor to the whole operation. If things went as he knew they would, the next time they took the field the influence of the warlords and shamans would be greatly reduced. He would gently remind Attila that it was he who had advised him to wait.

Undressing, he lay on his bed of silken cushions. Putting his head on his arm, he waited for the strong hands of the masseur. Wine was brought to him by a slave girl of China. She sat by his side and sang the songs of his homelands in a high lilting birdlike voice. He had paid a small fortune for her, but to have one of his own kind, even a slave girl, was a great luxury. At least he could talk to one who understood the graces of life. Yes, she was expensive, but he deserved it. Just because one lived in the field with savages didn't mean that one had to act like them.

Attila was receiving Ongesh's report. His chieftain was frothing at the mouth at the insult shown him by the Roman on the wall. He was just about to make a reply when his tent flap opened to admit one of his warriors, a Sabiri who threw himself on the carpeted floor, face down, hands outstretched in front of him.

Attila snapped his fingers for the man to make his report.

"Master of the World, I have just returned from a patrol and have seen a large formation of Romans on the march, heading in our direction."

Attila then proceeded to question the man about the numbers and their equipment and disposition. He was pleased that the Sabiri had seen no more than three legions of infantry and perhaps two cohorts of cavalry, along with some auxiliaries, slingers and some archers.

Attila immediately had several large patrols sent out to confirm the Sabiri's report. He dismissed the man, permitting him to crawl backward out of his presence, then told Ongesh to keep personal contact with the patrols as they returned and present him with the analysis of the situation.

In less than an hour Ongesh returned with a warrior of the Kutrigur who had been picked up by one of his patrols. Ongesh was in good humor as he kicked the man forward to fall on his face. "Tell the Master what you have seen and where you have been," he commanded.

The Kurtigur put his hands over his face in terror at being in the presence of Attila. Ongesh booted him in the side to get his tongue started.

The warrior's voice trembled as he blurted out his story. "Lord of Lords, I have just escaped from the Romans only this morning before dawn. I was held in their main camp for three days.".

Attila leaped to his feet. "You have been in their camp? How many? Were there any Visigoths with them or Franks? Who commands them?" His questions tumbled over themselves.

The report of the earlier scout was confirmed, but Attila wanted to know more. He leaned down to the man, grabbing him by the single long lock of hair hanging from the side of his shaved head. "What of the Germans and who commands?" he repeated.

"Lord, there were Visigoths and others there when I was taken captive. But last night, from where I was held with the other prisoners, we could hear a great argument going on between the Roman general and the chieftains of the Germans. The Visigoths left along with all the other German leaders. Swearing great oaths, they mounted and rode away, taking all their men with them. The Roman general was very angry. He cursed after them calling them women and cowards, that they would be forever dishonored among all the tribes and nations of the world."

Attila thought sucking his lower lip, his eyes dark. His face began to flush. "Who is the Roman general? I will not ask you again."

The terrified man buried his face in the carpet. "Lord, I heard him called Aetius."

Attila grinned with pleasure, this was even better. Not only had the Germans and the Romans fought but Aetius was commanding. That would make his victory that much sweeter. He still owed the Roman a debt that was long overdue.

Attila grilled the Kurtigur repeatedly, making sure of what he had seen and heard. Had there been any signs of any other tribesmen rallying to the Roman standard?

The man swore by the sacred sword that there had been no others with the Roman.

Attila grinned, laughing as he told Ongesh, "We have them. Three legions means they have thrown in their reserves. Defeat them and there will be nothing to stop us."

He had been concerned about the Visigoths and others allying themselves with the Romans, for that would have been the only source of enough cavalry to have presented any real threat to him. It was well; in one stroke he would break the Roman's back in Gaul, leaving the gateway to Italy undefended. He would have Rome.

Scouts reported back to him in a constant stream, giving him the direction and the rate of their march. Things were starting to move fast; he could be on them before nightfall. Orleans could wait. The city wasn't going anywhere.

He ordered Ongesh to call his warlords to him. Ongesh bowed his head in acknowledgment as he left to do his master's bidding.

Attila prepared himself for battle, calling for his sword and armor to be brought to him. He was fully dressed for war when the first of his commanders arrived. Then came the others; nearly all the great ones were there. His sons—Herna, the youngest and Arnak, his heir—and tough old Lauderrieks of the Gepidae. His kinsmen, Emnetzur and Ultzindar. Behind them were Elminger and Eskam, the shaman, standing beside Oebar of the Hundred Eyes. The last to enter was Donatus, the Roman deserter who commanded the siege machines and troop of foreign mercenaries from the Roman provinces.

Ch'ing was aroused from a half-slumber by his slave girl and barely managed to make it to the meeting before Donatus arrived. He was irritated at being notified so late. It was just another example of the insults he had to endure, one more injury he would have to pay back when the time came.

Attila strode back and forth. He was eager to ride. This damned siege had gone on for too long. Here was something he could deal with in terms he understood. Calling for a map, he pointed to the spot where they would meet the Romans. According to his scouts, the Romans should reach the place known as Lacus Mauriacus in the next couple of hours. He would be there to greet them. Attila nearly burst with eagerness; three full legions and their cohorts of cavalry—nearly forty thousand men!

Runners were sent to spread the word to mount and fall into formation. Ch'ing was not consulted on anything. It would have done no good anyway. He could see Attila had made up his mind. Therefore, he kept his own counsel. Full of foreboding, he returned to his quarters to prepare for the ride. He could have stayed behind but Attila might need him if anything went wrong.

It would give them more confidence if sacrifices were made and honor shown to their heathen gods. Aetius could ill afford to alienate any of his men at this point. They had to have full confidence in their coming victory. To ensure this, he had paid good gold to have the shamans read fair portents of the coming battle in the twisted intestines of sheep and the cracked shoulder bone of a white ox. Once this was done, he did notice that an edginess among the Germanic federati seemed to ease off a bit. They were more relaxed. A man who was going to face death needed to know that the gods were on their side.

There was nothing for him to do now but wait. He let the men rest in ranks with one rank always standing to in full readiness. Waiting was always the worst of it; however, if things went as planned, it should not be much longer, and already the sun was casting midday shadows.

Attila's outriders came back to him at regular intervals. He wanted a constant stream of intelligence about the terrain ahead. So far they had reported seeing nothing but dry woods and fields where no cattle grazed. The land was quiet.

Attila and his force were making good steady time, moving at an alternating rate of trot and walk. He would not have his horses worn out when they came to grips with Aetius.

He was still five miles from the Catalonian plains and Lacus Mauriacus when the first scout reported back to him that Romans were at the field and in ranks. The master of the Huns was pleased, but at the back of his mind, he still heard the warnings of Ch'ing Li. Ch'ing had been right too many times. He had his force draw up into squadrons. They would now advance at a walk.

He sent out still more fast riders to scour the countryside for any sign of Burgundians or Franks. The heat of the summer sun was enough to force sweat from pores, dry the mouth and start white streaks of lather forming on the shoulders and flanks of the war horses. The air was still. The dust that the horses stirred up formed into thin hazy clouds of sparkling motes swirling around the horde.

The command went out for all to prepare themselves. Bows were removed from shoulders, strings checked, swords loosened in scabbards, spears taken from their wicker carriers and laid across the bows of saddles. With the command went a familiar tingle of anticipation, the building of the urge to kill.

Riders returned from scouting more frequently. They had been far to the rear of the Roman force. The Roman was alone. Attila nodded his head in dark pleasure. It would not be much longer and he would have Aetius. From his skull, he would fashion a drinking cup of silver and gold, lay rubies in the eye sockets and have the teeth replaced with sapphires.

Ch'ing stayed in the rear of the Hunnish forces. He would move up when the battle began. He knew that at this time, Attila would most likely not listen to him, but he wanted to be close if anything went wrong. Then he might be able to save the day and restore his position when all others failed.

Ch'ing had a bad feeling about everything taking place. There was too much coincidence to suit him and he knew that Aetius was a shrewd commander, a thinker who understood the Hun mind. It was not like Aetius to commit the last of his forces at this place and time. But he would see. . . . If there was any blame this day, it would not fall on his shoulders.

He moved his horse and his bodyguard up into the gap between two groups of warriors where he would have more protection. He rinsed his mouth from a silver flask filled with spring water to cut the dust and longed again for the silken pavilions of China.

To the rear of Ch'ing, Casca and his small force of three thousand men moved after the Huns. He had to make up time and ordered his men to dismount and run along side their horses. There were two men to a horse, one hanging onto the saddle, one to the tail. This way he hoped to be able to reach the battlefield in time with his horses still fresh enough to do some good.

The men, he knew, would be all right if he could let them have a half hour or so to catch their breath, but between running and riding, both men and horses should be in pretty fair condition when they got there. He had learned this technique of long riding from the Huns.

He had to gauge the time perfectly. If he went too fast, the Huns would spot him and turn on his small force and destroy them. If he was too slow, he would be of no use when the battle began. His force was small, but often a few men at the right place and time could mean the difference between victory and death. He had to be on time.

He was concerned about the dust cloud that his force threw up and hoped that, as usual, the Huns were not looking back. Their eyes were always to the front when going into battle.

He gave the order for his men to mount and swung up in his saddle, staying to the front. Before leaving Orleans he had selected a hundred tough-looking regular army men to serve as his herders. They kept to the rear, making sure that none dropped behind or tried to desert. After they killed three stragglers, the rest got the idea.

Attila looked across the field where the Romans were lined up in what was obviously a defensive position. The stakes in the front could give him a few problems, but he knew that he had the numbers to win. The forest behind the Romans would slow him down a bit, but if he just took his time, he would be able merely to stand off and let his archers pick the Romans off one at a time.

Ch'ing had moved to the shade of a small grove of elm trees. He dismounted and had a blanket and cushions spread for him to rest on. He also had a good view of the battlefield. One of his guards served him wine of Syria in a paper-thin lacquer cup decorated with graceful scenes of waterfalls and swans. He watched the Hun force draw up, the hooves of their nasty-looking horses stamping the earth in impatience.

The men were as wild-looking as ever. More of them had armor now than when he had joined, but it was a wild mixture—whatever suited the individual's fancy. Skins of sables rested on the collars of shirts that nearly rotted away on their owners' backs. Swords with jeweled handles nestled in scabbards of filthy goatskin. The Germanic tribesmen that served with them were little if any better. The Gepidae were especially loathesome with their fair hair and large, uncouth, ugly bodies. They were nearly the equal of the Hun in their lust for plunder and slaughter, and the weaker the victim the better. They and the Huns were perfect soulmates in the act of ravaging. He had seen them once take a monastery and then whip the priests with strips of rawhide, forcing them to fight each other for the amusement of their captors.

A movement of men on the right side of the field caught his eye and brought him back to the present. It appeared as if Attila might be getting ready to make his opening move.

Aetius was as ready as he could be. Everything that could be done was. Now it was up to Attila. The movement of the Huns spreading themselves out across the field said it was nearly time for him to light the brush they had piled up in front of one section of the stakes. The brush was dry and had been liberally soaked with oil. But he would have to wait until the Huns began their attack in earnest. He walked the lines of his soldiers, giving words of praise and encouragement, letting himself be seen by all.

Aetius watched the skies and lengthening shadows. It had better be soon. If the Huns waited until it was dark, it would be too late for him to have any chance of victory. He had to get them moving.

Aetius called for a decaturion to escort him and one of his junior centurions out into the open. The decaturion was selected for his almost legendary lung power. At Aetius's command, he bellowed out an invitation for Attila to meet with them in parley.

Even from where Ch'ing was sitting, he could hear the decaturion's bellow and hoped that Attila would not take the offer. When Aetius wanted to talk, it usually meant someone was going to get the short end of a deal.

Attila responded to the offer to parley and kicked his horse out into the open, taking Ongesh with him. Aetius mounted his own horse and, with the junior officer, went out to meet with the Hun. The long-time opponents watched each other as they neared.

Attila was curious as to why Aetius would want to speak at this time, but he certainly had nothing to fear.

Aetius was a man of honor, there would be no ambush set for him.

Aetius thought about trying to kill Attila as they talked but just couldn't bring himself to do it. He had better stay with his original plan. If he was the one killed, then the whole operation would fall apart. There was more at stake this day than just his own life.

CHAPTER EIGHT

The two men and their escorts rode to a spot in the center of the field where they were easily seen by the warriors of both sides. Raising his fist, Aetius saluted Attila.

"It has been a long time since last we met, Lord Attila."

Attila reined his horse up and settled back in his saddle, eyeing his opponent. "This is true, Roman, but then we always knew that this day would come, did we not?"

Aetius nodded his head. "That's true enough, and I am glad we are finally going to get it over with. Though I will say that while I am going to regret losing you as an enemy, it will give me great pleasure to drag you in chains through the streets of Rome as part of my triumph."

Attila felt his face flush with anger. "You speak of chains, Roman. Never have I lost a battle and always have I taken the Roman in chains to do my pleasure. I was going to just have you killed, but now I believe I shall save you for other amusements."

Aetius laughed in his face. "You filthy savage, do you really think you can beat me? This time you are not

133

facing some novice and there are no traitors here to open the gates for you." He pointed back to his line of legionnaires. "I know you think you have the advantage of numbers, but I have the men. Men, do you hear me, not animals! My legionnaires are the pick of the Empire, each of them is worth ten of your filth-eaters. You unbelievably stupid savage. I am going to drag you in chains to Rome where your testicles will be removed and you shall crawl to the feet of the Emperor and beg to be permitted to kiss them as his dog."

Aetius ignored the paling of Attila's face and the barely controlled jerk that shook his body. Aetius spat at him. "That is for you and your filth. I only came out to see you one last time. In the event one of my men gets excited and happens to kill you instead of taking you prisoner, I wanted to see your face in order to remember just how incredibly ugly you really are. By the sacred blood of Jesus, there is no place in the world where any civilized race could call you by the name of man."

Aetius reached into his saddlebag, removing a flask of beautifully worked Byzantine gold. He whipped his horse around and tossed it to Attila, who caught the flask easily in the air.

Aetius rode off calling back to him: "My parting gift in case you work up a thirst this day. I know the taste will be familiar and welcome to you."

Aetius whipped his horse back to his lines, his sides nearly bursting with the effort to control his laughter. Aetius slid his horse into the protecting ranks of his legionnaires and finally let loose of his laughter. If what he had just done didn't get Attila moving, then nothing would. He knew that Casca would appreciate the gesture, for it was the scar-faced man who had told him of a variant of the trick being used with great success in

China, when a Chinese general had an opponent that he wanted to get into battle.

Attila remained where he was, stunned by the words of Aetius. Not even his father or brothers would have dared to address him in such a manner.

The golden flask sparkled in the afternoon sun. Curious, though still in a rage, he carefully opened the top flask and sniffed at the contents from a distance. Aetius was right, the aroma was familiar. He tipped the flask a bit and caught a golden drop on the tip of his finger and touched it to his lips. Attila screamed. Blind outraged fury ripped away all sense of caution. He flung the flask into the face of Ongesh, crying out, "Piss, that's what it is! That motherless piece of Roman filth has given me piss to drink!"

Attila whipped his horse back to his own ranks, drew his sword and cut the throat of a Utigur warrior who was too slow in getting out of his master's way. Attila was escorted back to his lines by gales of laughter from the Roman lines, as the story made the rounds.

He pointed his sword straight at the Roman ranks.

"Kill me those men, but not Aetius. He is to be taken alive. The man who kills him will be torn apart an inch at a time. Now *kill . . . kill . . . kill!!*"

The horde lunged forward in a mass, horses shoulder to shoulder crowding each other. There was no attempt at tactics, they would just try to roll over the defenders.

Aetius ordered the brush to be lit and a column of black, oily smoke reached straight up to the clear sky. "Now, the time is now. If we can just hold them for an hour."

The charge of the Huns was restricted by the tree line, which was in a semi-oval that channelized the attacking warriors as they drew to within bow range. Aetius ordered the ranks of legionnaires to step back until they were in the trees where they would have maximum protection from the flights of shafts which he knew would soon be reaching out for them. His own archers were already drawing strings back, awaiting the command to let loose their missiles.

The first barrage of Hun arrows flew in a cloud over the distance separating the enemies . . . ten thousand arrows reaching for the soft unprotected parts of the Roman defenders. The moment the Huns fired, Aetius ordered his men to form a modified tortoise in which the shields of the legionnaires formed a covering beneath which they would have some degree of protection from the flights of deadly shafts.

Most of the arrows did no harm, but even so three hundred men fell in the first minute of the attack. Aetius ordered his men to counter with their own barrage, but they were to aim at the horses, since they were larger targets. The archers did as they were commanded and soon the screaming of wounded and dying horses filled the air. Their mindless cries of pain were worse than those of their riders.

The Huns raced almost to the stakes before turning back. They had no desire to impale their animals on the hundreds of sharpened stakes. When the Huns neared the stakes, the first rank of legionnaires stepped forward and cast their javelins in unison, then immediately returned to their position in the tree line.

Attila had the first rank of Huns in the assault put to death by their comrades for stopping in front of the stakes and not pushing through. The Huns regrouped after their first flurry and hurled themselves and their animals directly onto the sharpened stakes this time. All this served to do, besides causing the death of several hundred of his troops, was to throw the Hun ranks into confusion as they piled on top of each other in their haste.

Aetius's archers had a field day. There was no way they could miss firing at the mass of wild screaming savages from a distance of less than fifty feet. Aetius held back the rest of his javelins. He would need them later and wanted to let the archers do their work now.

Attila finally gained a degree of control over himself and gave the command for his warriors to withdraw and regroup. He was furious with himself for falling victim to Aetius's ploy. He knew now that Aetius had deliberately provoked him into making precipitous assault. Well, he would not make that mistake again. He had the men and he had the time. The Cur-quans screamed orders and lashed their men with whips until they were once more in their proper groupings.

Ch'ing Li sat comfortably under his shade tree and dined on a meal of cold pheasant, which had been aged just the right amount of time to make the tender meat even more succulent, and watched the proceedings, content to wait until he was sent for, which, if Attila kept up his stupid frontal assaults, shouldn't be much longer.

Attila paused to consider his possibilities. He could send his warriors around the flanks and try to hit them from the sides and rear, but that would mean they would have to enter the trees where they would be the least effective. He gave orders for the Roman deserter, Donatus, to be brought to him. Donatus was a handsome man with clean features and gentle brown eyes. His manner was that of one wellborn, but that was a façade that hid a cruelty which even the Huns admired.

He seemed to take a special pleasure in the slaughter

of his own countrymen. He affected the costume of a barbarian, though he kept his face clean-shaven in the Roman manner. But in his actions, he was as vicious as the worst of the horde. His devotion to death and to Attila had brought him into the inner ranks of the war councils of the Huns.

He saluted Attila, waiting for his master to speak. Attila kept looking at the stakes. "Donatus, clear me a path through those stakes and I will give you first choice of the plunder of Rome itself."

That was all the encouragement Donatus needed. Plunder meant also the women of Rome. He would like to have a senator's daughter for a slave to humiliate in front of her own father. The Huns always said that Donatus had a good sense of humor.

He grinned. "Give me the Gepidae, Goths and others of the Germanic tribesmen and I will give you your path, Lord." Attila nodded for him to continue. "The Germans are better suited for what I have in mind, as they will have to move fast on the ground and their legs are better suited for the work I will need to have done."

Attila agreed, giving him permission to leave. The Roman traitor knew his job, which was why he had been given command of all the siege machines and heavy equipment.

Donatus gathered his force and sent them to collect bundles of dry wood and long grass. From Ch'ing Li he acquired some oil which would be suitable for starting a fire. The burning brush that Aetius had set in front of his stakes had given Donatus the idea of how to get through the barrier. When his force was ready, he had three hundred men from different tribes mounted, ready to advance. In front of them were three thousand Hunnish bowmen who would provide them with a screen until they were near enough to the stakes.

Donatus looked to Attila for permission to begin. It was granted. The Huns moved off at a gallop, then as they neared, they fell into full run. Even at that pace, the Huns fired their arrows with great accuracy as they spread out in a frontal line, speeding across the open field.

Aetius, from his position, could only see the Huns in front. He wondered why Attila was trying a direct assault again. It wasn't like him to make the same mistake twice. His answer came when the screen of Huns split to either side and the German allies of Attila came on until they were nearly on the stakes. Then they threw themselves from their horses, hurling their bundles of grass and wood onto the barrier.

Of the three hundred, half of them died in less than five minutes as the legionnaires cut the tribesmen down with arrows and javelins. But it was too late. The red coals in the pots had been blown into life and several fires were already catching and burning brightly.

Several Romans tried to rush to the barrier and beat out the flames, only to be cut down by Attila's archers. A path was being burned through the only thing which could keep the Huns off the Romans. Smoke billowed up, heavy and choking; luckily, most of it blew back toward the open field.

When the Huns separated, Donatus had pulled back to where he could watch from a safe distance, as the Germans set fire to the barricades. When the survivors turned to run back to the safety of their Hunnish allies, another fifty or so fell to shots in the back or brain. But they had done their job and the bowmen of Attila would see that no Roman would live if he approached the blaze.

Aetius was getting really worried. If help didn't

arrive soon, his ass would be in a sling. He tried to reassure his men as best as he could but he was uneasy, considering that his options were damned limited in number. He could pull back into the woods, but that would only delay matters a while. They would have to come out sometime and you could be sure that Attila would not let him get away. No! He would not give into panic and change his plan. He would stay where he was though he knew there were a hundred things which could go wrong and any one of them could mean disaster. But he would stay.

Attila was pleased that the fires were burning fiercely. Earlier, he had been cursing the dryness of the season. Now he was thankful for it. The wood was dry. Soon they would crash through to eliminate once and for all those in front of him.

He told Ongesh to place himself in the front of the main force. He was to have the honor of leading the final charge. He placed his sons on both the left and right flanks to command the wings. Once the center had fallen, they would dismount and go into the woods on foot, leaving their horses behind. From the shelter of the trees, they should be able to do good work, especially if the Romans were retreating as he expected.

The fires were burning down low; the acrid odor of smoke hung over the field. Attila moved to where he could be seen, raised his sword and pointed it at the ranks of the Romans. He raised the shining blade above his head and brought it down sharply. The entire Hun force moved forward, first at a trot, then a gallop, and finally at breakneck speed in a wedge formation. The wedge would punch through the opening created by Donatus, penetrate to the rear and fan out. The rest would follow in their wake as water pours through a funnel.

His allies from the Gepidae and Goths would advance with them, then dismount to fight on foot. They, too, would try to move to the rear, cutting off any escape by the Roman. That would keep them where his horsemen could still maneuver on the edge of the field.

The drumming of a hundred thousand hooves sounded like thunder over the fields. Twenty-five thousand Huns in the first wave rode like madmen, screaming wildly. Attila would hold the remainder of his force in reserve; that was one thing Ch'ing had taught him. Always keep a tactical reserve for the moments when things don't go the way you want them, even if everything looks all right. Never commit your reserve until you're absolutely certain they are needed.

Aetius had his bowmen take up a position behind the ranks of legionnaires who were standing firm, though he knew the horror that must be eating at them at the thought of being taken alive by the savages. Death was not what they most feared.

The first mass of Huns on the point of the wedge reached the burned-out stakes only to be met by a solid airborne barrier of missiles. Arrows followed spears, thrown from the hands of desperate men who had to make every one count.

Huns in the forefront went down. The rest crashed their horses into the front rank of the center, using spears, then swords, to hack a path through to the rear. Behind them their brothers were eagerly pouring through the gap which was widening more at every moment.

Aetius was hesitant about committing his cavalry,

but he had no choice. He gave the order for them to charge, though their numbers were pitifully weak. The Roman cavalry broke from the trees in a solid front. Spears held level with their hips, they hit the wedge in the side, driving into the center of it. They stemmed the tide for a few minutes until they were wiped out.

It was then that a new sound came to the ears of all who were not so blinded by battle that they could not hear. It was the roaring battle cries of twenty thousand Burgundians and Franks, followed by the Visigoths. Aetius nearly wept with joy. They had come, his ploy had worked. They had let the Sabiri tribesman escape after witnessing what would appear to all the final breakdown of relations between the Romans and their allies.

The Burgundians and the others had ridden off to wait for the signal from Aetius, which was the column of smoke Aetius had lit at the beginning of the battle. The problem had been that they had to keep moving farther away to avoid the outriders of Attila.

The Burgundians smashed deep into the right side of the Hun wedge; this time there was little room for bowmanship. The long swords and heavy axes of the Germans proved more than a match for the Huns at close range. As they beat the Huns back, Aetius gave the order to attack from the center with his infantry. He had no cavalry. All the brave young men had died, but their deaths had given him a few minutes more to await the arrival of the Germans.

His legionnaires gave forth their own battle cry, following eagerly behind. The legionnaires moved into the milling mass of combatants, using their weapons to good effect, slicing the throats of Hun war-horses or hamstringing them. Spears were used to lift many bodily off their animals, then to the ground where they could be properly butchered. But the Huns fought back fiercely, giving no quarter, asking none.

Ch'ing rose to his feet at this new occurrence. What he had feared had come true. Aetius did have something up his sleeve. Ch'ing didn't even bother to mount his horse. He ran across the field to where Attila sat stunned, watching his men die. Ch'ing screamed out at the top of his lungs: "The reserve, let loose the reserve or all is lost."

That snapped Attila out of his shock. He gave the order for the remainder of the Hun warriors to rush to the aid of their savage brethren. The battle swayed one way then another, always hanging in the balance . . . neither side could completely dominate the other. Then gradually the Huns began to pull back. Ch'ing was having a fit. Attila wanted to retreat and run but Ch'ing told him to form his wagons in a circle. From the inside, the bowmen would be able to hold off the Romans and their allies.

If they broke and ran, then panic would spread like wildfire. They would be hunted down and killed like wild animals. There would be no way to control a panicked flight. Attila knew Ch'ing was right and gave the order. The wagons he brought with him were formed into a large circle. Then he entered inside the opening left for his men. They withdrew, constantly fighting, until most of them had managed to break contact and were now behind the fragile sanctuary of the wagons.

The Romans and Germans were too exhausted to advance any farther. The tribesmen's long ride to the rescue had nearly worn out their horses and the fierce battle had drained both them and their animals of most of what strength remained in their arms. They were willing to call a halt to the fight for the time being and give both men and horses time to regain their strength and treat their wounds.

Casca saw the smoke before he heard the sounds of battle. He formed his men up into two columns with a force of five hundred set into two ranks at his front, forming a T.

A group of several Huns broke out of the trees, running in a panic. They didn't see Casca and his men until they were already face to face. In the lead was one of Attila's Gepidae leaders, Lauderrieks. Casca met him head on with a steady hand. He hurled his short throwing spear straight into the Gepid chieftain's chest. The blow punched a hole in the breastplate of embossed iron, knocking him from his saddle to lie dead on the ground, mouth open, eyes staring at nothing. Casca's horse trampled on his face as they advanced against the rest of the escaping Huns.

The Huns wanted no part of any more fighting at this point and most of them managed to escape to race off in different directions. Casca's men wanted to track them down, but he refused them. He couldn't take a chance on having his force broken into separate wandering groups he couldn't control. He might still be needed at the real battle taking place in front of them. Though the fact that Huns were fleeing the field was a good sign, it didn't mean that it was over or even that Aetius had won. Things could turn around faster than a pimp could sell his sister.

When he reached the field, there was less than an hour of daylight left in the sky. His men joined the forces of Aetius and were made welcome. They were absorbed into the ranks, filling out the places of those who had fallen on the field. They were put with the rest of the army into positions surrounding the Huns in the circle of their wagons.

Aetius clasped Casca by the shoulder, hugging him in delight. "By glory of God, I am glad to see you, my friend. For a time I didn't think you had made it." Casca filled him in on the events that had taken place at Orleans.

Aetius was elated at the news. "Good, good, my friend, then we have done well this day. Rome shall live for a while longer."

Casca followed him to his tent which had been moved closer to where the Huns were now barricaded, stating, "It was good to see the tables turned in our favor for once. The Huns have had their way for far too long."

As the sun set, Casca rested beside Aetius, sitting on a field chair outside the tent. The sounds of the aftermath of battle reached them from a dozen directions—the groans of wounded men who were being treated by physicians and the sounds of graves being dug for those who had fallen.

Casca pointed out a glow coming from the Hun position where campfires were being lit inside the circle. He roared with laughter when Aetius told him of the trick he had used on Attila to get him mad enough to charge. Neither Casca nor Aetius could know that Attila was in a fit of depression and the fire they saw was from the burning of saddles of horses which Attila had heaped up in the center of his circle. Attila was determined that before he would let himself be taken prisoner, he would throw himself into the flames.

The glow they watched that night was the burning of many of Attila's dreams. If they had made one more concerted attack that night, Attila would have died on his funeral pyre. But they and their men were too tired. The final battle would have to wait until dawn. Then they would see about putting an end to the ravages of the Huns once and for all.

Strong sentries were kept on all posts that night and horsemen slept by their animals, ready to mount at a moment's notice. They wouldn't take any chances on being surprised. The Hun was wounded but he wasn't finished. Nearly twenty thousand were still left alive and that was a formidable force to contend with, as the Romans and their allies had only slightly more in their ranks. The battlefield of the Lacus Mauriacus was theirs but the victory was yet to be finalized.

Ch'ing Li had to talk himself blue to get Attila out of his fit of self-pity. "Lord, you would not heed my words, but don't give up. We will still have our day. Now listen to me and this is how things shall be done. I will not let you fall."

Without speaking, he listened to Ch'ing and finally began to perk up a bit. It was true; they had been fought to a stalemate here, but there were still huge numbers of men to call on if they could break free. Once they left Gaul behind, it would not take more than a few months for him to gather another large army from the hundreds of tribes in his domain.

He listened eagerly to Ch'ing and even said to himself that he would not again go against the advice of his faithful counselor.

Ch'ing Li spent most of the night with Attila. It wasn't until two hours before dawn that he came up with the solution to their problem. At this point, Attila was ready to try anything. He had never been in this condition before—where he was the one surrounded, waiting for the enemy to attack at dawn. When Ch'ing Li explained his plan, Attila snapped at it, anything to get out of the confining rings of the wagons.

The orders were given. They would have to leave

their wagons and their supplies behind, but this was a desperate time.

One hour before dawn, the Gepidae and the Germanic warriors formed into a single force. Attila gave them their orders. They were to assault straight through to the tent of Aetius. There they would kill the Roman general, leaving the Romans without their brain.

The Germanics loyal to him were to be his spearhead and given the honor of leading the way in the breakout. At the signal given by Attila, they burst out of the rings of the wagons and rushed straight into the Roman ranks. The Romans were not found sleeping and quickly fell into formation to resist the attack. But in the confusion of the dark, they thought the entire Hun force was on them. The Romans and Visigoths on the south side of the encirclement came to their comrades' aid.

When they did, the Huns, instead of backing up the Germans, left them on their own and headed south through the weakened lines of the Visigoths. Attila leading the way, Ch'ing Li close behind him, they broke through with little difficulty and rode away from the fields of Catalonia and Lacus Mauriacus.

Their loyal allies were quickly cut off and surrounded by the superior Roman forces and butchered. But Attila was free and away. There was no way the Romans would be able to catch him. The seven thousand Germanics he had sacrificed meant nothing to him. The important thing was he had managed to save the heart of his forces and himself. The lives of a few oversized barbarians meant less than nothing.

But to those dying, the name of Attila was cursed a thousand times before the last of the Gepidae fell, his mouth filled with blood.

The Roman forces had reacted so quickly to the attack from the Gepidae that there had been no time for Aetius to give orders. He and Casca had to simply join into the melee and fight alongside each other in the dark until there were no more bodies to strike out against.

The greatest disappointment was when they found the camp of the Huns empty and knew that Attila had fled. They were not yet through with the Hun. Aetius and Casca knew they would have to do it all over again. But their victory this day would give new heart to the Western Empire. The Hun could be beaten. This was the first time, and both men swore it would not be the last.

As the sun rose, the bodies of both sides littered the field, broken and useless. The losses had been nearly equal so that it could not be called a great victory, but at least they held the place of battle and had forced the Hun to withdraw. The psychological benefits alone were worth the loss of life. . . . At least they were to the living.

Casca walked over the field; the terrible aftermath of a desperately fought struggle was all too familiar. For a moment he wished for the quiet and forgetfulness of the marshes, but he knew he couldn't hide from the world forever. Sooner or later, no matter where he was, the world and its struggles would force themselves upon him.

He found a place to sit on a small grassy knoll covered with the high dry yellow grass of summer and sat thinking about what life was all about. He gave up trying to find an explanation that could justify the thousands of lives taken by fate in the last hours.

CHAPTER NINE

Attila sat upon the ridge overlooking the battlefield he had just left. His deep-set eyes, black as chips of obsidian, showed no sign of the anger which was beating within him. He had lost. His first defeat—was it an auger of things to come? His horsemen and their allies were streaming past him heading back the way they had come. Those who were severely wounded or on foot were doomed. He knew their heads would lie before Aetius by the next dawn. The horsetail standards swung listlessly in the evening breeze.

Whipping his horse around, he turned from the scene of his failure, unconcerned about the thousands of his warriors being put to the sword by the victors. That night, as the wind blew through the coals of a bronze brazier, he waited for the man he had summoned.

Silent, he brooded over his loss. He had been sucked into a trap and had to recognize it. The one he was waiting for entered on his knees. Ch'ing knew when to play the part of a truly submissive and loyal servant. In his hands he carried the rice paper scrolls which had brought Attila one victory after another. Snapping his fingers, Attila called for wine of Persia to be brought. Ch'ing considered this a bad sign. Rarely had Attila ever taken much to drink other than the harsh fermented mare's milk that served his poorest tribesmen. Ch'ing hoped that this was not going to become a habit. Wine was not good for the heads of savages. They had no tolerance for civilized beverages; it made them crazier than they already were and much harder to deal with.

"What went wrong, scholar?" The question was not spoken threateningly. He wiped a drop of wine from his thin beard. Again he asked, "What was my mistake, scholar? I know you warned me against coming to Gaul in the first place, but we should have won even with the Visigoths and Franks riding against us."

Ch'ing nodded, affecting his most safe manner. He gracefully unrolled the scrolls and set them before Attila.

"You lost because you would not listen except to your own desires." Ch'ing was careful to use tones which were not accusing, only statements of fact. He handled the scrolls lovingly; as always, he admired the artistry of the author and the graceful techniques used in the calligraphy of Sun T'su's *The Art of War*.

Ch'ing looked through the scroll until he found the passages he wanted. He was always careful to have Attila feel that what was said came not from him but from the writings of a man dead a thousand years. In that manner, the anger of Attila could be deflected. He was merely the tool that interpreted the scroll.

"Lord, you have made three errors. First, it is written, and I have read this to you before, that one never takes the field for more than one season if it can be avoided. Second, never become involved with long sieges; it debilitates the men and exhausts the fields. Third, never give in to anger, for emotion is like the clouds of the moon. By that I mean that the mind, when clear, is the moon in full light. It can see all in startling clarity. But, when the mind is filled with anger, it becomes clouded and conceals the face of the moon and you are in darkness where you cannot see your way.

"You have been in the field for three seasons without rest. The siege of Orleans went on too long. And lastly, when the Roman insulted you, you lost your temper and acted in haste on a field of battle that was not of your choosing. All these things you did against the teachings of Sun T'zu."

Attila was nothing if not a realist. He knew Ch'ing Li was right. He had lost his temper when Aetius gave him the flask. He would remember the bearer of that obscene gift for a long time.

He questioned Ch'ing further, "What about the trap and the manner in which we were lured away from the walls and the lie about the Visigoths and the Franks not being with the Romans?"

Ch'ing thought about it for a moment. "Lord, the trap and the technique used in getting us to fall into it resembles one that is in the book of Sun T'zu, also. There is a story in my land of how a gift was given to another with the same unfortunate results. It is an old, old tale in my country. Perhaps we are dealing with someone who has read the same book we use."

He stroked his mustache with manicured nails. "I believe I know who it is that has been giving advice to Aetius. All of this began when a rider entered the walls of the city yesterday. Then, when Ongesh and I went to deliver your ultimatum, we were received by a man with a scarred face. It was he who insulted Ongesh and broke the truce. Also, it was he who led the forces from the city which attacked us from our rear.

"If that is so, then we will have to be careful in the future and hope this scar-faced one does not gain too much power. The writings of Sun T'zu will serve all who heed them. I feel that we are not through with the scar-faced Roman."

The old legend from his homelands touched at Ch'ing Li's thoughts. *Could it possibly be? The Roman did bear the marks the legends spoke of, both in his eyes and scars. But how could one live for such a time? The stories did say he had been touched by the gods. What if . . . ?* His superstitious speculations were interrupted by Attila rising from his knees and heading for the entrance to his tent. He was stopped by a discreet cough from Ch'ing, who had been brought back to the present. "We have another problem, Master."

"What is that, scholar?"

"Lord, it is imperative that we keep your reputation for invincibility unblemished. We must put the blame for this defeat somewhere else. We have to give someone to the men or they might lose their faith in you."

Attila thought that over. It made sense. "All right, I'll go along with that. But who?"

Ch'ing concealed his smile. "I have already considered our needs, Lord. It must be one who is always in their minds and is close to you. One thing all armies have in common is complaints about their rations, and we have been on short supplies these last months. Also, he should be the one who advised you to undertake this campaign and even convinced the other chieftains to join with him in his arguments."

Attila stopped his pacing. "You mean Ongesh?"

Ch'ing nearly burst with pleasure. "Yes, Lord, it must be him."

Attila shook his head. "But it is not Ongesh's fault that there was a shortage of food. You know the countryside had been gleaned down to nearly the last kernel of grain before we ever set foot here, and what they didn't harvest they burned. It was impossible for the land in such a condition to support such an army as mine for an extended period. Even with those problems you know that Orleans would have fallen in a few days. Should I hold Ongesh responsible for my mistakes?"

Ch'ing agreed, "Just so, Lord, but his death would serve two purposes for you. It would give the men renewed faith in you and also be a salve to their pride. They will readily accept short rations as the reasons for their defeat. It is vital that this be done."

Attila shook his head. "Ongesh has been with me from the beginning, always at my side when I needed him. He is like a brother to me."

Ch'ing smirked behind his bland features. He recalled what had been the fate of Attila's own brother

Ch'ing bobbed his head in agreement. "Just so, lord, it has to be one that the men know you have great love and respect for. To put the blame on someone of no importance or that you dislike would have no value. It must be someone you are fond of. That will prove to the men that not even your personal likes will deter from doing that which is just and proper. And if I may remind you, we did come here because of Ongesh. It must be him or perhaps one of your sons."

Attila rose up at that. "No, I am not going to kill one of my sons. At least not yet anyway. So be it, scholar, we will talk again later. Leave me now and send in Bardov, the captain of my guard; if this thing is to be done, it must be handled quickly."

Ch'ing bowed from his kneeling position. In obeisance he performed Kowtow, touching his head to the floor of the tent. This was one time he wouldn't mind obeying Attila's orders. Gloating, he rose, backed out of the tent, pleased with himself. He had just repaid one of the scores he had to settle, and with Ongesh out of the way, the others ought to be even easier.

Attila ate cold horsemeat, washing it down with

kvass, chewing and swallowing slowly until he heard Bardov beg for permission to enter his presence. When it was given, he saluted to his master and awaited his orders. Attila told him to bring Ongesh to him, then leaned close to his man's ear and whispered. Bardov heard his master's voice. "I hear and obey, Lord."

Attila finished his cold horsemeat by the time Bardov returned with Ongesh and had shown him inside, then left to take up his place, guarding the master's tent, satisfied that he had obeyed all his master's orders, even those whispered in his ear.

Ongesh, his scarred, knotted, high-cheekboned face attentive, stood expectantly in front of Attila, waiting for him to speak.

Attila spat a piece of horse gristle from his teeth before talking. "Ongesh, what are you?"

His chieftain responded, "I am the property of you, my Lord."

Attila watched him carefully. "And is all that you have not mine?"

Ongesh sensed that something not to his liking was taking place. He fell to the floor, touching his head to the carpet. "It is, Lord."

Attila picked his teeth with the point of a dagger. "Good, then we are in agreement. Old friend, I have need of your head. It must be shown to the tribes in order to restore their confidence in me. You are being permitted to serve me in the most important way I know. You shall take the blame for today's defeat by the Romans."

Ongesh swallowed bitter bile. "Is there no other way, Lord?"

Attila shook his head in regret. "No, my old friend and comrade. It has been well thought over and decided. It must be done that the tribes retain their faith in me."

Ongesh raised his eyes to look at Attila. He saw no hope in them. He took a deep breath. "Then I am honored that I shall be permitted to be of service to you once more. May I ask what will become of my sons and wives?"

Attila grunted in approval. The custom for men who failed was not only to lose their lives but also those of their families.

Gently he eased his old friend's mind. "They shall be well cared for and honored. Your sons, when they are of age, shall become Hetmen and Cur-quans and trained along with those of my own blood. The tribes shall be told that you came to me voluntarily and demanded that I take your life in recompense for your failure to provide properly for them and for your bad council in coming to Gaul at this time. Such an act will be respected and honored. No touch of shame shall reach your family. On this you have my sworn oath."

Ongeth lowered his face back to the floor. "Thank you for your kindness, Lord. When do you wish my head?"

Ongesh remained, his face to the carpet. He didn't see Attila raise his fingers and signal to the shadows. A figure stepped forward, swinging with a two-handed, heavy, thick-bladed sword. The head of Ongesh rolled free from its trunk to rest at his feet, eyes looking blankly into those of his friend and master.

Attila sipped his wine. "Now, old friend, now." He ordered the executioner to remove the body. He was, after all, not a cruel man. This way Ongesh died without giving him time to think about it and perhaps do something foolish as men are prone to do when faced with their own termination. Yes, this was much kinder than having him publicly executed.

He regretted his loss, but Ch'ing was right as usual. The times he had chosen to go against his advice had usually cost him.

Ch'ing had served him well over the years with his advice. It was he who told him that a body with two heads will always be at odds with itself. Shortly after that he had killed his brother Bleda.

He knew Ch'ing had been a councilor to the court of the Emperor of the Eastern Chin but had to leave the court for reasons he never spoke of. Attila had quickly learned the little man had a reason for everything he did and said. He knew that Ch'ing served him for his own purposes and that was the way it should be. A man who does not seek power is fit only to be used by those that do. They could be of greater value than those who give only blind obedience if you understood them. But one day the little man would be right one too many times. . . .

CHAPTER TEN

It was disappointing to them that they were not able to follow after the Huns, but they had been too badly hurt themselves to continue and they didn't have the same impetus that the retreating Huns did. And there would still be mopping-up operations to take care of for the next few days. In the woods there would be some survivors that got separated from the main force.

Casca took his men back to Orleans, bringing the wagons of the Huns with him, bearing their wounded and whatever goods had been left in the wagons, which were considerable. And in the Huns' main camp outside Orleans, magistrates had counted and weighed over two thousand pounds of gold and five of silver.

When Aetius's troops reentered the walls, it was as heroes. The news of the defeat of Attila and his army brought the entire population out into the streets.

Casca was content to leave most of the glory to Commitus who rode at the head of the column. Once they were inside, he broke away and went to his house, where he lay down and slept the deep rest of the soul-weary.

The pounding in his mind was distant but insistent. It would not stop; it kept pulling him up out of the dark where he wanted to be. At last he gave in and opened one eye, then forced the other to do likewise. Grumbling, he rose, covered his naked, scarred body with a thin coverlet of cotton, and stumbled to the door. He felt like he had a hangover of the first order. He slid the bar back and swung open the door. The sudden burst of bright sunshine from the outside momentarily blinded him. He squeezed his lids shut, then opened them more slowly to focus on the person disturbing his rest. Words were already coming out of his mouth before his vision cleared enough to make out that he was talking to a woman.

"What, by the waterlogged gonads of Neptune, is it now? Can't a man even get a few hours of damned sleep without some stupid—" At that point his eyes fully focused on the small, dainty figure standing in front of him. Her face was dominated by the largest pair of eyes he had ever seen—dark brown eyes that were so deep a man could drown in them. Her face was framed by a wealth of rich auburn hair that hung in waves to her shoulders.

He coughed, embarrassed. This was a lady of quality. "Forgive me, domina, I didn't expect one such as you to be beating on my door."

The voice that snapped back at him had enough poison in it to kill an Egyptian cobra. *"Your* door, you vulgar savage. This is my home. Where is my family?"

Casca gathered his thoughts, shook his head to clear away the cobwebs. "Your family? Oh yes, certainly. Please come in."

She pushed past him, followed by a stocky figure he hadn't noticed before standing out of sight at the edge of the doorway. Janus, her servant, gave him a dirty look as he followed his mistress inside. He was very protective of his young charge and thought of her as his own. Janus had been her tutor and confidante for most of her life.

Casca moved out of the way of the small balding man, nearly tripping over his own feet in the process. The girl turned her attention to him again. "I am Sylvia Rhea. Now where is my family? And who or what are you?"

Casca remembered the bodies he had buried in the garden at the rear of the house when he had moved in. Haltingly, he tried to find the right words but knew there would not be any that would make the telling any easier.

"I am Longinus, a soldier. I wish there was some other way to tell you this, but there isn't . . ."

Sylvia stopped him. From his tone, she already knew what he was going to say. "My family is dead?" The voice was very tiny, almost a child's.

He nodded his head. "All of them." He watched the tears welling up in her eyes. "All that were here. When I came to this house, I found three people—a man with gray hair and a mole on his cheek, a woman and another young girl. I buried them in the garden." He answered what would have been her next question before she spoke. "It was plague. I am sorry, Domina Sylvia, there was nothing that I could do. They were already dead and had been so for several days."

Sylvia was in a mild state of shock. The news of her family's death was not completely unexpected; but it was still hard to hear the words that they were really gone, all of them. It was unfair. God could have at least let one of them live.

Casca excused himself and went to his room to change. He had nothing there but his blood-stained tunic and armor. The armor he left off, but wished there was something he could do about the dark marks on his tunic. In a corner of the room, he went through his saddle bags and found a thin blue cloak that, while well-worn, at least didn't have the marks of death on it. Covering his shoulder with it, he pulled it over to conceal most of the stains.

When he returned, Sylvia had herself under a tight rein. "Now, where is my family?" she commanded. Casca, as meek as a lamb, led her to the rear of the house and the garden. Sylvia watched the broad back in front of her. *Why is he here and who is he?* She didn't know whether to be angry at him or not.

In the garden between flowering bushes and under the shade of two giant poplar trees, she saw three mounds of raised earth; on their graves were blooming flowers.

Casca coughed self-consciously when she asked about the flowers and who had planted them there. "I did, domina. It seemed the thing to do and no one else came here. All the people of the city were afraid of the plague."

Tears welled up and over her lids to run down her face, but there were no cries of grief. Pain of this kind was personal and private. She would let her feelings go when she was alone, not in front of a man she didn't know.

There was a nice quality about him, though. His appearance was a little frightening—the muscled neck and scarred arms. She looked closer at his face and wondered about the scar there. But in his face she saw no brutality, only something behind the eyes that said he too had known the pain she felt now.

"Thank you for the flowers. That was a kind thing to do. But I would appreciate it if you would leave me alone now." She knelt down by the graves. "Tell me who is under which of these places." She couldn't bring herself to say graves.

Casca called them out in order . . . father, mother,

daughter . . . then turned to leave her to her grief. It was always embarrassing to watch another's pain when you couldn't do anything to help.

He returned to his room to gather his things together. He would have to leave now. Her servant stayed by the door watching to make sure he didn't take anything that belonged to the house.

By the time he had gathered his few possessions and was ready to go, Sylvia had come back inside. She looked at him questioningly. "You're leaving?"

He nodded. "Yes, now that you are here, I think it would be best if I found somewhere else to stay. But I would like to know how you got here so fast. The city was only secured yesterday."

She looked at him as if he were a fool. "Yesterday? It has been three days since Commitus returned from defeating the savages." *Three days!* He had been asleep for three days. Well, what did it matter?

He only said an embarrassed, "Oh! I didn't know I had slept so long." He took his gear and moved to the door, opening it. "If there is anything I can ever do for you, I would consider it an honor for you to call on me. Any place and time. Perhaps there is some way I can repay you for the use of your home. Remember my name is Casca Longinus; you can find me at the military barracks."

She merely nodded her head. He left her there looking small, frightened and lonely. The door closed behind him and he was in the street.

He looked up at the sky. From the shadows, it was still a few hours until nightfall. In his sack was his armor and a couple of changes of clothing that needed a washing. The streets were busy; several caravans of carts bearing foodstuffs passed him. Obviously, supplies were coming into the city at a good rate as no one was trying to steal anything from the carts. It was a good sign of normality returning. He did see many houses boarded up, most of them probably victims of the same plague that killed the family of Sylvia.

It took about half an hour to walk the two miles to the military barracks where he called to a young junior centurion and ordered him to find him a room. The young handsome officer looked very smart in expensive armor that hadn't any marks of battle on it. But from the way the young man moved and the glint in his eye, Casca figured that that would probably change before very long.

He took Casca's sack and led him down a hall in the stone building that served as the legion's facility. He opened a door into a fair-sized room of about fifteen feet square with a desk chair and sleeping couch. The youngster stated that the room had belonged to an officer who had been killed.

Casca checked it over. There was nothing left in the wooden closet or elsewhere. The room had been cleaned out. Tossing his bundle of dirty clothes at the centurion, he grumbled, "Have someone clean these and bring them back to me in the morning." He was saluted and left alone.

He had an orderly bring him water to wash in and some food, nothing fancy, just a portion of boiled millet and stewed pig. Chewing slowly, he let the food find its way into his gut with the least amount of protest.

The girl refused to leave his mind; her large eyes kept peering at him. Well, he thought, she's nothing to me, just another pretty face that I will never see again. I have no business even thinking about another woman. All I can give them is grief and do myself no good in the process.

He lay down on the cot, trying to think about what he should do next, but he was restless. His thoughts of the girl didn't help. Finally he gave it up and belted on his sword to go back out on the streets. Before leaving, the young centurion, who was officer of the day, told him to be careful. There were still a large number of looters roaming the streets after dark.

Casca asked him about what measures were being taken by the legionnaires to provide security. The boy responded with, "There just aren't enough of us left to patrol everywhere. We have caught over fifty and they have been executed. After a while we'll have their numbers thinned out so we can handle them better."

Casca asked, "What do you mean there aren't enough of you to deal with the situation?"

The centurion pointed at the inner barracks; most of the bunks showed no signs of occupancy. "Aetius has taken over fifty percent of the able-bodied men with him. We have nothing but a skeleton force left, and the praetor has most of them on the walls still watching for Attila and his hordes to come back."

Casca left the centurion to his duties. He didn't like the sound of looters, those human vermin who fed on other's misery. But they always came like flies; wherever there was death, they would appear as if by magic. It had always been so and he imagined it would always be.

He let his feet take him where they wanted, not really knowing the streets well enough to make a decision. He wandered until dark fell. There were no torches lit to illuminate the dark narrow streets, but he could hear sounds behind shuttered windows and voices talking. Men arguing with wives. Children being told to shut up and go to sleep. The familiar sounds of civilization.

The streets were rapidly emptying. The good folks were locked up in their houses for the night. Most of them still had the look that only extended hunger can give. Soon the only sounds he heard were those of his boots on the stone streets. A city that lives in fear has a feel to it that is unique. It's not anything you can touch or see, but there is a quality to the atmosphere, a tenseness that hangs on through the night.

He gripped the handle of his sword a little tighter. One of the few good things about a city that's been under siege is that its rat population is diminished—once the inhabitants get over their food prejudices . . . He saw, or thought he saw, only a couple of the rodents.

Only once did he see a three-man patrol of legionnaires on the streets and they acted like the last thing they wanted to do was meet up with any looters. He didn't blame them—they would probably be outnumbered. He identified himself to them, received their salute, and they went on their way, leaving him to the darkness.

The narrowness of the streets made the night seem even darker, even though there was a full moon whose rays darted in thin shafts between the structures, illuminating a pile of rubble here or child's toy there, where it had been dropped and forgotten.

Several times he heard noises that weren't those of the tiny scuffling feet of rats; other vermin were on the streets this night. He moved over to the sides of the buildings, staying in the shadows where the moonbeams couldn't touch him. He felt a chill and turned around; the building he was in front of had a familiar look to it.

It took a moment for him to recognize it in the dark. It was the home of Sylvia. Somehow his subconscious had brought him back to this place. He thought for a moment about knocking on the door, trying to think of some excuse that would justify his being there but gave it up. He turned away and moved on down the street away from the home of the girl with the haunting eyes.

He got three doors down when he stopped. His feet

just didn't want to take him any farther. He wished he had a drink, but if there was a tavern open, he wouldn't know how to find it, and there wasn't anyone out that he could ask.

Casca resigned himself to being a little tense and sat down on the curb, his back against a wall, just watching the cold rays of the moonbeams as the orb slowly traveled over his head. He pulled his thin cloak about his shoulders. Though there was no chill to the warm night air, he felt as if there ought to be one. A light wind overhead rustled the leaves, blowing several off to float gently down to the street.

It wouldn't be much longer before all the leaves began to fall and another winter would be coming. He wondered where he would be then. He reclined against the baked bricks of a house and closed his eyes, letting the quiet of the night sink into him. It felt good just sitting, but he had a vague uneasiness that kept him from fully relaxing.

A sound of heavy steps snapped his eyes open. He cocked his head to listen. Nothing for a moment, then he heard it again. A tingling ran up his spine to the small hair on the nape of the neck. He rose, slid his sword from its scabbard, and tried to fix the sound.

He moved around to the side of the house, stopped in the dark of the shadows and listened once more, holding his breath to hear better. He heard a grunt and a muffled curse, a sliding noise, then one more. Moving on, down the back of the houses, in the gloom, he saw a dark figure pulling another up over a wall. Doing a mental count of the houses he had passed, he knew they were going over the garden wall of Sylvia's home.

Silently he followed after them, when they dropped over the top into what he knew was the garden. He waited a moment, then did the same, easing himself over belly first. Making the smallest possible figure in the dark, he let himself down silently onto the grass. He was just a couple of steps away from the graves of Sylvia's family. He strained his eyes looking for the men. He couldn't see them, but he knew there was only one way for them to get into the house without having to climb up to the second floor and that was through the atrium door. He headed there, walking carefully.

The door was open and he knew they were inside. Sliding in sideways he stopped, listening for footsteps or the sound of their breathing. Moving to where the stairs led up to the second floor and the upper bedrooms, he hunched down in a darkened corner where the moonlight couldn't reach. It was pitch black. He waited, knowing that sooner or later the looters would have to come to him after they finished checking out the rest of the bottom floor and found there was nothing there worth taking.

He was right. It was only a few minutes before the shuffling of their feet and a muffled curse, as one of them bumped his hip on the sharp corner of a table, came to him. They knew that there was someone in the house from the food they had found in the kitchen. Their steps came closer. He set his sword down by his feet and took the wide-bladed dagger from his belt. It was better for close work in the dark. There! He saw a darker form. He waited until it passed him. The man in front was going up on the stairs on tiptoe; the other had a club in his hand. He presumed the man in front had some sort of weapon, but he waited until the trailing man was just at an arm's reach away, then moved when the leading man was nearly at the top of the stairs.

Casca's hand choked off any cry from his victim's mouth as he pulled the man in close to him. He slid the dagger, with the flat side of the blade up, deep into the man's body and just under the lowest rib on the right side, then turned it into the left to sever the spinal cord. There was nothing but one long exhalation to mark that the looter's spirit had fled this vale of tears.

Picking up the dead man's club, he moved up the stairs after his victim's partner who had halted. He heard a low angry hiss to hurry up and grunted an unintelligible response. The thief on the top of the stairs thought he was his partner. Casca grinned to himself. He went up the stairs two at a time. When he reached the top, the looter was at a door. He motioned for Casca to come closer.

Casca thought, *You're not going to like this.* He moved up right behind the man, raised the knob-ended club and came down, cracking the man's braincase. He caught the body before it hit the ground. He didn't want to wake up the girl. She had been through enough. He lowered the body and started to drag it off when he stopped. Setting the corpse down, he stood at her door for a time trying to make up his mind.

Not really aware of what he was doing, he opened the door and entered, closing it behind him. He could see her lying on her bed, a thin coverlet pulled down to her waist. A glow from the moon filtered in through a small window set high on the wall, illuminating her face. He moved closer, fearful that she would wake.

In the night glow there was an ethereal quality to her. He bent over her, careful not to let his shadow touch her face. He just wanted to look at her. Her hair was loose, lying in waves about her. One breast was exposed where it had slipped out from under her nightdress. Well formed and ripe. He touched her hair with his rough fingers, feeling the texture. It was finer than the rarest of the silks of Chin.

He was tempted for a moment to put his hand on her breast to feel the warmth of her, but he couldn't do it. He didn't want to have her awake and find him standing over her. No, it was best if she never knew. He pulled her coverlet up gently and slipped back out of her room, stopping only for one last look. He shook his head thinking, *It would do no good even if I could make her love me. What purpose would it serve?* The memories of past loves and the pain of them were too great. *This time I'm going to leave before the hurting starts.*

He picked up the body of the looter, threw it over his shoulder, took it out to the garden and tossed it over the wall, then went back for the other and did the same with him. Once he had them on the other side of the wall, he dragged them by their heels, one in each hand, two full blocks away and left them one on top of the other to be picked up with the rest of the city's trash.

He returned to his room at the barracks, but his eyes refused to close all that night. It wasn't until dawn that he finally rested for a few hours. When he rose, he had made up his mind he was going to get the hell out of Orleans before his will weakened. He found his clothes had been scrubbed as per his orders; he cleaned himself, dug out his razor and scraped off the growing beard.

Once he was reasonably presentable and in full armor, he went to the headquarters of Commitus. Not waiting to be announced by the praetors's orderly, he just went on by him into Commitus's inner sanctum. Commitus was reading dispatches from Rome and the adjoining provinces when his uninvited and unwelcome guest entered.

He was irritated at the intrusion, and his voice made his feelings about Casca quite clear. "I don't believe it is asking too much for you to have yourself announced in a civilized manner."

Casca merely put one of his buttocks on Commitus's

desk and leaned over. "Knock off that crap. I'm not in any mood for it. All I want from you is to know where Aetius has gone and if there have been any reports of Hun activity in the region."

Commitus gave him a sour look, replying, "As to your questions, Aetius has been recalled to Italy for a conference with the Emperor. However, before he left he gave me orders to tell you if you ever showed up again to come to him by the fastest possible means. He will be at the court in Ravenna. As to the second part of your question, no! There has not been any sign of Huns in the area and if there were, I assure you that I am quite capable of handling the situation without any assistance from you."

Casca smiled at Commitus. "That's really good to hear. I mean, how you can handle things; you were doing such a good job before I came. I will never forget how eager you were to leave your walls and do battle with the Huns face-to-face. Yes, sir! You're a real killer. Now give me a requisition for a horse of my choosing and some money, about a thousand denarii will do for my expenses."

Commitus nearly swallowed his tongue. "A thousand denarii?"

Casca stopped him before he could make any further comment. "That's right, and I don't think you will have any problem finding it, or would you prefer for me to tell Aetius about the several wagons with your personal guards driving them—the ones that veered off the main street when we brought back the spoils from the Huns' wagon train?"

It did his heart good to stick it to a prig like Commitus every now and then. His requests for horse and money were filed in record time. He had the thought that in order to get him out of the city, Commitus would have paid three times that amount gladly. But it was not good to be too greedy.

He turned his gelding to the southeast and let the horse pick its own speed. Whatever was out there waiting for him would still be there when he arrived.

The journey on the road to Ravenna was uneventful. He passed several lines of troops, both federati and Roman, some going north but most heading south to Italy. The defense of Gaul had been turned over for the most part to the Burgundians and Salian Franks.

He reached Ravenna by the end of September. Casca didn't have very fond memories of Ravenna and the last time he had been there. At least the fanatic religious fervor of the Christian zealots seemed to have waned a bit.

He only stayed long enough to find out that Aetius had moved his headquarters out of the city and was staying to the north, close to the Julian Alps. Casca figured the reason for that was if Attila came again, then it would probably be from the north as the experience of fighting in Gaul had probably left a bad taste in his memory. Few leaders ever liked to fight again where they had lost a battle.

At Altinum he wasted a few days relaxing. He had started to feel like his old self and decided it was time to get his head on straight. The best cure for the doldrums he knew of was a healthy period of strenuous, nonthinking exercise spent in the fleshpots. He left about half the money he had taken from Commitus there with the girls.

On the way out of Altinum, he considered his curse and decided it wasn't all bad. There were a few fringe benefits to it. One was that diseases kept their distance from him, even the pox. He might get ill for a while but it never lasted.

At a small fortress at the north end of the Po Valley, he caught up with Aetius who was looking fit, tanned and ready for action, if a little tired. He still had problems in Rome getting the Senate to agree to do anything other than half measures. He was concerned that if they didn't send him more men, the Huns would simply flank his position and drive to the rear as they had done often enough in the past. Intelligence reports that had come in indicated they had been right in thinking that Attila would come again.

Attila had moved remarkably fast in gathering another force. Aetius knew that in the spring the tribes would begin to send their fighting men to the standards of the Hun. Attila would come and this time the fight would be handled differently, of that Aetius was sure. He still felt he could beat him, but he had to do it on his own terms and in the place of his choosing. That would be impossible if all he could do was react to actions initiated by Attila. He had to gain the initiative from the beginning or they were in big trouble.

CHAPTER ELEVEN

Ch'ing Li was not pleased with Attila, but there was little he could do. He was only permitted to give advice when asked for it and, of late, anytime he didn't agree with what Attila already had in mind, he was quickly shut up.

Things were not going as he had planned since they had left Gaul. True, they had rebuilt their armies from the nearly endless supply of manpower the steppes and wild lands had to offer. But Attila had insisted on starting raids against Illyricum and the provinces held by Emperor Marcian. That would mean trouble in the long run for he knew Attila planned on invading Italy in the summer.

Ch'ing was becoming disgusted with the Huns; they would not listen. Like petulant children, they had to do everything their own way. The losses they had suffered in Gaul had killed off many of their best warriors. The recent raids had regained much of the confidence of Attila's men by pillaging several minor provinces. Ch'ing had advised against them at that time for they could force the Eastern and Western Roman Empires to join forces. But Attila would have his way and Ch'ing knew he was determined to try for Rome.

As Ch'ing's difficulties with Attila increased, he began to doubt whether he would be able to use the Huns as a tool of revenge. The savages were just too stupid. If they refused to listen to him and take his council then he knew that disaster would most certainly not be far away. Since the battle at Mauriacus, Attila had taken to drink; his confidence was shaken. Ch'ing had to constantly reinforce his ego with words of praise. Too often he had found the master of the world lying in pools of his own vomit surrounded by his drunken chieftains. *Animals!*

Ch'ing was disappointed, but he had invested too much precious time to give up completely on the Huns. He would stay with them for a time longer. Perhaps, if things went well in Italy, he would be able to direct their energies toward his ultimate goal: the conquest of Chin—where he would force the Celestial Prince to crawl on his belly before him. It would please him greatly to see the pride of heaven lick his boots. Then all the rest of the nobles who had plotted against him would be made to pay. The thought of those soft decadent fools who had conspired to drive him from the court to this place sickened him no less than these ignorant Huns and their filthy habits and diet.

It was almost more than he could bear.

He would spend hours trying to decide which would cause them the most pain. For some it would naturally be of the physical nature, such as being torn apart between horses or being delicately dismembered, one tiny slice at a time with red hot razors; for others, he would destroy their pride and their minds by forcing their wives and daughters to lie with savages while their husbands and fathers watched.

Ch'ing Li sighed deeply, returning from his pleasant reverie to his current difficulties. Why would Attila not heed his words? With his council, they could have the world. Couldn't the fool see it was too soon to take the field in a major campaign? And the political atmosphere was not to his liking. He was still bitter when Attila summoned him to his tent where he was brooding.

"Sit down, scholar." The term of respect made one of Ch'ing Li's plucked eyebrows go up. That meant Attila needed something.

"Thank you, my Lord. How may this unworthy one be of service to you? It has been several weeks since last you called me to your council."

The self-deprecating tones of Ch'ing Li didn't fool Attila. He knew the little man was pissed off because he wanted to take the field against Rome. Ch'ing didn't understand that he had to beat Aetius to restore not only the confidence of his warleaders but his own.

He still needed the brain of Ch'ing Li and the writings on the scroll he carried with him. He could have taken the scroll from him, but he knew he could never find one to interpret it as Ch'ing Li did.

Attila motioned for Ch'ing Li to take a seat. He leaned forward intently. "You know my plans for the invasion. What do you think the odds are for success?"

Ch'ing decided to try once more. "If you go against Rome now, I do not think you will win." He spoke rapidly before Attila could interrupt him, "You will have some degree of success, but the secret will be how far to go and to know when to quit."

Attila didn't like the answer and while he was determined to do things his way, he still respected the intelligence of the man sitting before him. "What do you mean?"

Ch'ing Li phrased his words very carefully. "Marcian will go against you. This time perhaps he will even attack you from the rear while you're tied up in Italy. There are still tribes that do not love you well and would rally to the Romans if they thought you had any chance of being defeated. That would mean great difficulties for you.

"Also, as I have said before, it is not the time. You should wait, but I know you have made up your mind not to." Ch'ing Li paused to catch his breath. "Just remember, once we are committed, we must be very careful not to become bogged down or we will suffer a worse fate in Italy than we did in Gaul."

Attila prodded him. "What do you mean by accepting a degree of success and knowing when to stop?"

"Lord, there will only be one way to know that condition and that is when we face it. Sun T'zu makes it clear that there are some battles to be fought and some to be avoided, some roads to take and others to avoid. We will most surely come to those two conditions and we must recognize them or suffer disaster."

Attila was concerned about the possibility of Marcian sending forces against his rear. That meant he had to leave large formations behind him to protect his lines of communication. He would give orders for his armies on the eastern borders of Constantinople to make all the signs of a major war but only to hit and run. Just enough to make Marcian think twice before committing large numbers of troops to the battle in the West.

It would tie him down securing his own frontiers if he thought there might be a simultaneous invasion of his lands. By the time Marcian found that he was not facing the Hun main force, the battle for Rome would have come to a successful conclusion.

Ch'ing just wouldn't understand. He had to invade or those of his tribes that were disillusioned by the defeat in Gaul would claim he was not strong enough to keep his power. There were some who would sit in his saddle. The only thing that his warriors respected was strength. If he showed any weakness or hesitation to act, he would be eliminated. Therefore, he had already laid the groundwork for the destruction of Rome, and after that, Constantinople would fall to him.

The call to gather the horde had been sent to the furthermost reaches of his domain. The tribes came: the Gepidae and Alans, the Goths and Sabiri, the Unugar and Utigur, the Kurtigur, Abasgians, Rugians, Sclaveni, Alpicur, Acatziri, Hunuguri and the Geticae. These and a hundred others sent their warriors to obey their master's will. The horde of Attila was ready.

The order was given. He bypassed the strongholds in the Julians and struck deep into Italy. Nothing opposed him. Countless villages were put to the sword, their people either killed or enslaved. Fire and the sword spread the message of the Hun's arrival. By comparison, the Goths of Alaric had only been weekend tourists. Everything in front of the Huns was destroyed. What they didn't take was burned. Captives by the thousands were taken from the valley of Isonzo, where they were used as beasts of burden to help carry the plunder of their new overlords.

Aetius could offer no real resistance in the Julians; all his force could do was conduct a fighting withdrawal and holding action. That could not stop the Huns, but it did slow them up. Aetius needed time, time for those fools in the Senate to finally give him the manpower he had asked for months ago.

Attila had things the way he liked them. His confidence returned. This was war the way the Huns loved it. There was a prize he wanted before going after Rome itself and that was Aquileia. It was too rich and too strong to leave in his rear. It had to be taken.

Ch'ing nearly gave up in disgust when they looked down the walls of Aquileia. True, there was tremendous wealth inside those walls. Aquileia was nearly as rich a prize as Rome itself, but Ch'ing knew that, like Orleans, if they didn't breech the walls in a matter of days, the price for the city could prove too high.

He nearly pulled the hair out of his head in frustration. What was this fascination that Attila had with walls? The strength of the Huns rested in mobility and long-range strikes, not in sitting before some damned wall watching your horses eat up the fields.

Attila knew what Ch'ing thought; he had been told often enough. But he needed to take a major walled city as part of his plan to regain the total confidence of his war leaders. The other side of the coin was that if he took Aquileia, the Romans would know he could do the same to their holy city, too. These things made it vital in his mind to do whatever was necessary to breech the walls.

Attila stayed with the forces attacking Aquileia, which consisted of seventy-five percent of his total manpower. The rest of his warriors spent most of their time scouring the countryside for food and sending it back to their brothers outside the walls.

For nearly three weeks the defenders held the city. The Huns were wearing out. Even with siege machines, they had not been able to make a hole through which they could assault.

Attila was at the end of his patience. If the walls didn't fall soon, he would have to leave Italy and withdraw. He could not keep his men tied up in this one spot much longer. He knew that every day they wasted here gave the Romans under Aetius time to plot against him.

Attila was riding around the perimeter of Aquileia with Ch'ing Li at his side. Ch'ing Li knew that his master was in trouble and it was difficult for him to ask for advice at this point. Ch'ing Li might have been content to leave things as they were, but he too was committed now and had to do his best to see if the campaign couldn't be brought to at least a partially successful conclusion.

Those behind the walls couldn't be in much, if any, better shape than the Huns. The city would have to fall soon. Ch'ing Li hated the idea of the siege to begin with, but now they had gone too far to back out of it. Attila, like any savage, tended to sulk and do things on impulse, especially when things didn't go the way he planned them. He had thought they would be inside the walls in less than a week.

Ch'ing reined his horse up, raising his eyes to the sky, shading them with his hand. Attila looked up to see what Ch'ing Li was watching. Ch'ing pointed with an inch-long manicured fingernail. "There, do you see them?"

Attila searched the sky. "See what?"

Ch'ing Li pointed again. "The birds—the storks are leaving the city. There is our answer."

He then told Attila of the story of Lu Kuang who conquered Turkestan for Fu Chien. In February 384, he brought the city of Ch'iu-tz'u under siege. The city resisted him furiously, repelling all his attacks until he was in a state of desperation. That night he had a dream in which a golden image flew over and out of the city. Kuang said to his men, "This means the Buddha and the gods are deserting them. The Hu shall perish."

Attila understood that Ch'ing Li was drawing a parallel between the dream of Lu Kuang's flying Buddha and the storks which were leaving Aquileia. Then it hit him, and for the first time in weeks, he smiled, then laughed. This was what he needed to inspire his men for one last great assault.

That night, seers read the burned cracked shoulder bones of sheep for omens, all of which were favorable. Then he had the horde gathered, rode to a ridge top and looked out on the thousands of faces.

He spoke, giving them the message of the gods, "The storks who build their nests in the gables of the houses of Aquileia are leaving and taking their young with them. You know that storks are birds which have the gift of prophecy. They are leaving because the city is doomed. It is ours if we will but take it. On the morrow watch the skies and heed the message of the birds. When they fly, we attack!"

At dawn the entire Hun force was waiting, seventy thousand eyes watching the skies over the city for the storks to fly. Donatus had his siege machines ready— several large battering rams and a hundred and fifty platforms of his own design.

The new platforms were ones which could be carried piecemeal, dragged behind riders to the wall, then manhandled into position until they joined together one section on top of the other to make a structure high enough to reach the top of the walls. Then they would assault directly over across a small drop bridge device which would also serve to protect those on the structure until they were ready to cross over.

On the ground he also had several hundred large shields covered with hides from which the Hunnish archers could be protected from counterfire from the walls. With these to give support to the assault force on his portable castles, they should be able to get over and into the city without unreasonable losses.

For the rest there were over five hundred ladders ready. With these preparations, the defenders would be hard put to deal with them all at the same time.

Ch'ing pointed to the sky. Two small white specks were circling the rooftops, then they headed due south. Then another three, then several more pairs. The storks were leaving.

Attila pointed to the birds. "Now!" he cried. "Now is the time. Give me the city and all that is in it is yours!"

The Huns rushed forward; the entire army moved against walls. Mindless of losses, they hurled themselves at the walls, hurling ladders against the barrier. Nothing would stop them. Not cauldrons of boiling pitch or water, not arrows, spears or pikes. Four thousand died in less than thirty minutes, but the portable castles were put up and the bridges dropped. Huns scrambled over the bridges to take the parapets. Behind them came the next wave like ants on a stalk of cane. They poured up and over.

When the first castle dropped its bridge, Attila knew the city was his. It took nearly an hour before his men managed to fight their way to the gates and drop them to give his cavalry an opening to charge through into the interior of Aquileia. Once that was done, there was no stopping them. It took four days and nights for the Huns to be sated as they took their revenge on those who had resisted them.

They stabled their horses in the temples of the Christians. No one was safe from them, not children or crones. The screams of women filled the skies and echoed from the walls of burning buildings. The men who were not of noble family were herded back to slave pens or killed. The rich could always be ransomed for a profit.

The city was put to the torch and walls torn down before they finally left, their wagons heaped high and heavy with the spoils of their victory.

Only Ch'ing was not pleased or even satisfied. The more plunder and slaves they acquired, the slower they would be able to move. He begged Attila to at least kill the captives, but even this reasonable request was denied. Attila could not tell his men to give up those which would show them a profit, and the others were needed to haul the baggage.

Attila was satisfied with his handiwork. He had restored his faith in himself. Other cities were taken but never with the devastating results and punishment he inflicted on Aquileia. Now, by the time he reached the city, its citizens had already run off, taking with them everything they could carry. But there was always plenty left behind.

Ch'ing kept after Attila to quit wasting time on looting, but the sight of the wagons of gold was too much. Attila couldn't get himself to bypass a city with full coffers. The taste of wealth he had taken from Aquileia was too great. From that one city he had acquired two thousand pounds of gold and six of silver.

Attila was full of his own power. He knew there was nothing that could stop him now; he would have it all.

Before he reached the Appenines and could enter the South, Aetius began his counterattacks, striking at the rear of the Hun columns, using the same whiplash tactic favored by them.

Where he hadn't been able to spare the men to guard all the passes in the Julian Alps, he could cover the narrow gorges of the Appenines. When the Huns were busy with the sacking of cities, he sent fast riders ahead of them, carrying the torch, to burn every field and orchard that could give the Huns food. Livestock that couldn't be driven away was slaughtered.

Best of all was that Emperor Marcian had finally

decided that Constantinople was not going to be attacked and had sent reinforcements to land at ports where they would be in front of the Huns.

At Medilanum and Ticinum, only the priests and clergy were put to the sword. Attila found it was taking too much time to slaughter the entire populations and they were beginning to have a hard time feeding their own without having thousands of starving slaves to hinder them. Attila began to feel with a sense of urgency that perhaps Ch'ing had been right again.

Casca was given command of a troop of light cavalry, one of those sent to the front of the Hunnish forces to burn fields and slow down the Hun advance. The plunder they carried in their wagons was the best ally of Rome, for the Huns slowed to little more than a snail's pace in their advance. All of this Casca and Aetius used to good advantage.

Near Tricinium, Casca and his horsemen entered a village whose people had died, not from the swords of the Huns, but from an enemy even more terrifying— *plague.*

Casca's men refused to enter the village or even dismount. Leaving them on the outskirts, Casca rode in alone to see if anyone still lived. The streets were littered with bodies, many lying in their own excrement where they had literally shit themselves to death. All had the look of bodies grown old before their time, wrinkled skins, sagging flesh and swollen tongues.

Only the dead were left. Casca wiped the dust from his face as he searched door to door, but there was no one there. If there had been survivors, they had already left.

The heat of the day parched him. He stopped and drank from a pot of water on a doorstep. It felt good to cut the dryness of his mouth. He looked for another two hours without finding anyone, then headed back to his men.

Casca was only a hundred yards away from them when he felt a stabbing in his guts—a cramp that doubled him over. He stumbled into a wall to hold himself up. One of his men started to help him but was held back by the others.

They were afraid to move another foot closer. Casca felt his bowels let loose at the same moment his stomach emptied itself on the dirt. He pitched forward to the street writhing in the dust in pain as his guts tried to tear themselves apart. He rolled in his filth, unable to stop the pain; his face was flushed, his tongue swelled to where it threatened to choke him, forcing its way partially out of his mouth. He bent at the waist then jerked straight out in spasms he was unable to control.

His men were helpless to do anything. They watched him in his agony for half an hour; finally he was still. They knew he had died of the plague. Whipping their horses, they raced from the village, leaving him there with the rest of the dead.

It was night when the leading element of the Hun main force neared the village. Attila was pushing; he needed to make up time. He didn't plan on stopping for another three hours yet.

Ch'ing was riding beside him as they entered the dead place. In the shadows they saw several bodies lying still in contorted positions. Ch'ing called for a torch to be lit and brought it to him. Raising it above his head, he carefully dismounted and moved over to get a look at the corpses.

Holding the torch down, he saw the face of a man in the uniform of a Roman centurion. Hissing between his teeth, he called Attila to him. He pointed to the face with the swollen tongue lying in a pool of dried vomit.

"This," he whispered to Attila, "is the man from the walls of Orleans, the one who led the attack on our rear at the fields of Catalonia. I remember him because of the scar on his face. See how it runs from his eye to the corner of his mouth." Ch'ing chided himself for being foolish and even considering the remote possitibility that this was the foreigner who had served the Emperor Tzin over a hundred years ago. That man was obviously and most certainly dead.

Attila poked the body with his sword, pricking the cheek. There was no doubt about it, the Roman was dead. "What killed him?"

Ch'ing moved away from Casca to examine several other bodies. He hissed and backed away, covering his face with his hand. "Plague," he hissed. "They have all died of the plague."

Attila didn't waste any time; he was back on his horse and riding away before Ch'ing could drop the torch and get to his own mount. They moved away from the village as fast as their horses would take them, leaving the rest of the column to catch up when they could. Attila was not going to stay near any place where the sweating death was waiting.

The Huns took a wide detour, but several of them couldn't resist going into the village to see if there was anything worth taking. They found food and drink still sitting on tables; this was worth the risk. They had been short of food for days and his the loaves of bread and wine beneath their tunics. Several of them drank from the village well and filled their waterskins with the cool fluid not knowing they were filling them with death.

Within two days a thousand of Attila's warriors had died of the sickness and more were showing symptoms.

Attila kept the sick away from him, leaving them in their own wagons with orders to stay away from the rest of the force.

Now they turned their faces back to the north away from Italy. Aetius picked this time to make an attack in force. He struck at the extended lines of the Huns with the reinforcements sent him by Marcian. They kept up a constant harassment of the Huns, freeing several thousand captives.

With the plague in front of him, Aetius hitting his flanks, and more of his men falling to the disease every day, Attila was faced with some hard choices.

Ch'ing was angry; once again Attila wouldn't listen to him. He would agree with everything he said, then go ahead and do things his way. There was no dealing with a mind like that.

Attila knew that he couldn't take Rome now. All he wanted was a way out before the plague struck him, too.

The Senate in Ravenna picked this time to once more interfere with Aetius and the conduct of the war. They convinced the Emperor to send a delegation to the Hun King and ask for peace.

Aetius was fit to be tied when he found out that Pope Leo had agreed to meet with Attila. With him would be the ex-counsul Avienus and the ex-prefect Trygetius, two of those who had interfered with his plans every time they got a chance. If it had been anyone other than the Vicar of Christ, he would have stopped it. But there wasn't any way he could fight the Church.

CHAPTER TWELVE

A tremor started in his right leg, stopped, then started again. The shaking moved up his body into his chest where the heart gave one tentative beat, then one more. He coughed. Out of his mouth came a green slime that flowed out under its own power. Sweat poured from every pore. The trembling increased until his whole body was shaking uncontrollably.

Casca opened one sticky eyelid, then the other. It took several minutes before he could focus them. The trembling began to ease but he was weak, terribly weak. It was hard to breathe; his chest felt as if bands of steel were wrapped around it, trying to cave in the bones. It took four hours before he was able to get to his knees, then slowly to his feet, to stand wobbling on trembling legs that threatened to go out from under him at every moment.

Casca's stomach tried to turn inside out, but there wasn't anything in it, only the vile taste of the green phlegm that had drained from his mouth. Staggering over to the wall, he dropped the bucket in and laboriously hauled it back up. He stuck his whole face in the water, sucking in the fluid, then poured the remainder over his head. He was still alive. His body had rejected the cholera baccili.

He was still disjointed in his mind and wandered through the village until his legs wouldn't hold him up anymore. Stumbling into an open doorway in the dark, he saw a bed and fell into it, unaware that he was sharing it with the corpse of a woman three days dead.

When he woke the next morning, he was barely able to rise. But after finding his face buried in the breast of the corpse, he found the strength to get the hell out of there.

The sun stung his eyes. He had to keep them half clenched to be able to see. He went back to the edge of the village; naturally, there was no sign of his men but he did see the marks of many horses on the ground. From the shape of the hoof prints, he knew that a large party of Huns had been this way, but the tracks didn't run on through, they must have turned back.

Casca moved on to the road, head aching with what, had he not known otherwise, he would have sworn was the grandfather of all hangovers. After walking about five miles he heard a thin whinny coming from some brush. Going to inspect, he saw that his horse had gotten its reins snarled in the limbs while trying to eat.

Well, finally, he thought. *A little damned luck for a change.*

He freed the horse, climbed on the saddle, and headed back for the road. He knew there was a spring located only about ten miles away. There he would be able to clean off some of his filth, and by then perhaps be able to eat something from his pack.

At the spring he did the best he could with himself but thought the odor of the sickness was probably going to be with him for some time. But he did get the worst of it off and felt better when he was able to eat a little cheese and a few olives, which aided in quelling many of his stomach's protests.

He slept again, this time until the next dawn. Rising, he

moved his horse to where it could find some grass to eat.

He wondered how things had been going since he had gotten sick. He didn't blame his troop of cavalry for getting out of the area. He just wished he knew this part of the country better. Saddling his horse again, he headed back to the road, hoping to make a connection with a Roman scouting party before he ran into any Huns.

He heard a thin distant sound in his mind . . . a droning, then a tinkling of bells. Thumping the side of his head a time or two to try and clear out the sounds didn't help much. It just gave him another headache and the bells kept getting louder. He had just about decided that he had lost his mind when he saw horsemen approaching him from the south. He pulled over to wait, trying to make out if they were Romans or Huns.

The rider bore an olive branch in front of him. A messenger of truce going to parley with someone. He waited until the rider was even with him, and then said, "Would you mind telling me what the crap is going on here and where you come from? Don't you know there's a war going on?"

The messenger was from the court of Ravenna, a young officious man who took his duties very seriously. And this crude and foul-smelling centurion addressing him didn't look like any that would ever be invited to dine at the palace.

"I," he began, speaking through his nose, "I am part of the escort of the most holy father, Pope Leo, on a mission of state."

Casca didn't like the young man very much and he still felt a little ill. He grumbled to himself, *If that snotty little bastard doesn't watch it, I'll put him in a state, a state of shock when he pulls my foot out of his ass.*

"Who did you say? Pope Leo?"

"The bearer of the olive branch asserted that was so. When Casca tried to pump him as to just why the Pope would be this far out in the boondocks, he received only a snotty, "Ask him yourself if you dare."

The sound of the bells and chanting became noticeably louder. The papal party was just a few hundred yards away.

"I *will* ask him, you little faggot," he countered.

A squad of ten richly accoutered papal guards were in the lead. Behind them came a double line of fifty monks on foot swinging censers and chanting. Several of them had bells in their hands. Behind them came a horse-drawn litter covered with gold leaf. In it was the most Holy Father Pope Leo, the Vicar of Christ on earth. Casca whistled between his teeth.

The Pope was dressed in full regalia, wearing his high crown and robes of silk embroidered with gold and silver threads. Jewels were formed into crosses on his cape. On his ring finger, he had a ruby big enough to buy half of Persia.

Casca shook his head. "I always thought that Christians were supposed to like being poor."

He really didn't want to have any dialogue with the Pope if he could avoid it, so he pulled up alongside the decurion in charge of the mounted escort. "What's going on here?" he demanded.

The decurion wrinkled his nose at the sour odor coming from the centurion. He didn't like it, but the man did outrank him. He answered stiffly, "we are the emissaries going to meet with the King of the Huns."

Casca whistled again between his teeth. "If that don't beat all, sending a Christian pope to try and deal with Attila. This I've got to see." Casca pulled into a place near the rear of the escort, keeping to himself. He had the feeling that if Leo was going to meet with Attila, then Aetius wouldn't be far away.

They traveled that day and part of the next until they came to the place agreed upon, in the Ambuleian district of the Veneti at the ford over the Mincius River.

He was wrong; there were no other Romans there, but across the river were nearly ten thousand Hun warriors camped and waiting.

At the approach of the Papal party, the Huns sent out one of their chieftains to wait on horseback in the center of the ford. The little faggot with the olive branch went to meet Harmatta. They were not by any stretch of the imagination a matched pair. At any rate, they had their talk and then went back to their own sides to speak to their principles.

There was a rustle in the crowd of Huns on the opposite bank and three men rode out. Casca recognized two of them right off. One was Attila; the other looked like the one who rode beside the Hun chieftain at the walls of Orleans.

Attila stood in the center of the ford on horseback. He wasn't going to give an inch. If the Pope wanted to talk to him, then he would have to come halfway.

Ch'ing had been whispering in his ear, "Remember about knowing when to leave. If we can break off this engagement and keep what we have taken, then it will still be a victory. There is always next year and treaties are made to be broken. We can always find an excuse to cry foul on the part of the Romans."

When the Pope came forward on his horse-drawn litter, he was still seated on his throne, holding up staffs topped with jeweled globes mounted with crucifixes. Pope Leo crossed himself as the brothers swung their censers back and forth, keeping up their monotonous droning chants.

Casca moved his horse closer to the Pope, who gave

him a questioning look, but seeing that he wore the rank of centurion, he didn't say anything.

Together, the horsedrawn litter and he on horseback, they entered the ford. The two leaders, one of a religion that preached peace and love, forgiveness of the enemy and mercy, faced the man who lived by taking what he wanted over the bodies of those in his way.

Attila was not displeased that the most powerful priest of Rome had been sent to parley with him. He hated Christians but knew the power Pope Leo would have over the politicians of the Senate. Whatever deal he could make with Leo would stick and he hoped to stick it to them properly.

Casca stayed to the rear on the right side of the Papal wagon. He listened to them bicker back and forth. From the concessions Attila made, he knew the Huns were in trouble and it was probably as Aetius had predicted.

The Huns were caught between the armies of Aetius and Marcian. They'd had their lines of communication severed and were short on food. From where he was, he could see that several of the Huns didn't look like they were feeling very well. He wondered if the plague had hit them, too.

Pope Leo and Attila were reaching some agreements when they came to an impasse. Leo lost his temper, stood up in his wagon, and began to preach at Attila, promising him eternal damnation. Then he got on to the power of Jesus and the resurrection, how only God could give man eternal life. Unintentionally, he pointed at Casca with his staff when he said this and drew the eyes of both Attila and Ch'ing to him.

They stared open-mouthed, their faces pale with fear. They had recognized him as the dead man they had left lying on the streets of the plague village. There had been no doubt that the scar-faced centurion had been absolutely and completely dead. Attila had put enough men into that state to recognize it.

Leo kept on about immortal souls and life after death. Casca just grinned at the man from Chin and his master. Casca didn't know why, but he was making Attila and his advisor very nervous.

Ch'ing tried to tell Attila that it was a mistake, that the man they were looking at wasn't the same one. But Attila knew better, and if the Pope could bring this man back to life, then who could tell what other magic he might bring down on him.

At this point, they came to a rapid agreement. Attila would release his captives and leave Italy immediately, never to return. Pope Leo was delighted that he had made Attila see the light. He wanted to spend more time with the King of the Huns, but Attila wasn't about to hang around any longer than necessary. He made a polite farewell and returned to his camp.

Within minutes, a stream of captives began to cross over the ford and the Huns were already pulling out, heading back north. Leo sent messengers to find Aetius and the commander of the forces sent by Marcian to tell them not to interfere with the passage of the Huns.

Aetius was furious with the deal made by Leo, but he was helpless to do anything about it. He had to stand by and watch Attila take his men out of what should have been a death trap had he been given a few more weeks.

Casca just wondered why the Hun and the man from Chin had been so startled at seeing him.

The hordes of the Huns retreated. They swarmed back through the passes under the eyes of their enemies who were helpless to do anything against them. It was frustrating to watch their hated foes leave, taking with them their plunder. The watchers also knew that in the masses of warriors were hundreds of citizens, mostly women, who would never be given back. Hardened soldiers wept at their inability to do anything to free their women; but the Pope had spoken and to disobey his word was to invite excommunication and the loss of their immortal souls.

In the lead was Attila, accompanied by his heir-apparent, Arnak, and Ch'ing. The latter was anxious to put as much distance between them and Italy as possible, and for much the same reasons as Attila. The scar-faced man who was dead, yet lived, was a sign that they must turn their faces elsewhere. Every day on the trail leading to the vast plains of the Hunnish domains, he continued to pound at Attila the need to turn east, away from Rome and her gods.

Attila's temper grew shorter in direct proportion to the amount of wine and kvass he consumed. He did start to regain some of his confidence the farther they went into his lands. By the time they had reached the valley where he gave orders to pitch his tents, he was full of both renewed courage and alcohol. He managed to convince himself that the Romans had pulled some kind of trick on him—that the man with the scar was not the dead man in the village. After all he had taken only a quick look at the corpse, and surely there must be hundreds if not thousands of men with scars on their faces and light eyes. No! It was not fear of the scar-faced Roman or their ruling Pope that made him stop his attack; it was the plague, and when the plague ran its course he would move once more against Rome. He would have the city and nothing that Ch'ing, that spineless coward, said would divert him from what he desired.

Ch'ing Li knew he was right, and if he was to save the Huns from themselves, he had to make Attila listen or all his work of the last years would be for nothing. He kept after Attila to change his mind at every meeting. Even when he knew that discretion would have been better, he kept on and on, like a gnat buzzing around a man's face, constantly annoying and irritating him, until finally Attila slapped his gnat down.

CHAPTER THIRTEEN

Ch'ing Li was in a rage, his face pale, jaws clenched to hold back the pain. His torn silk robes were slashed nearly to ribbons and the edges were stuck in the cuts on his back. Never had he been treated in such a manner—and by a savage! Once in his tent, he fell onto his couch, screaming at his slave to bring clean water and cloths to cleanse the wounds he had received for being honest with Attila. This was too much to endure. Who did that beast think he was to treat him this way? Had Attila forgotten that it was his brains that had led them to the brink of total victory and Attila's that had nearly destroyed them?

His slave treated his injuries as he fumed and plotted. Perhaps it was time there was a new master of the Huns, one who would be more pliable and willing to follow his advice to the letter. For the next three months he made a point of being very friendly to the sons of Attila. If there was to be a successor, it would have to be one of them. He waited until the propitious moment arrived.

Attila spent most of his time in his cups drinking the sour, potent kvass with his chieftains. Ch'ing Li knew he was reverting back to the pure barbarian, seeking the company and council of others of like mind—men who only knew how to kill, but would never understand the art of ruling.

The moment he had been awaiting came when Attila, in a drunken stupor, had taken the whip to Arnak. In front of the chieftains, he beat his son until the blood ran in streams from his face. Attila mocked him for being a woman and not fit to have the title and rank he, his father, had given him.

Arnak had offended his father by suggesting that perhaps it was time to draw back for a season or two and let the Romans alone. Give the Romans time to think they were safe so they would fall back into their normal custom of fighting among themselves and at the same time letting their armies deteriorate again. Once this happened, then they could go for the grand prize again.

Attila snapped open his brown eyes, red-filmed from drink and swollen nearly shut. His body began to tremble. He rose from his couch and beat Arnak, cursing him for being a coward, screaming that no one would stand between him and Rome, that he would have won if he had not listened to those who filled his thoughts with doubts. Well, there would be no more of that. Any who even spoke of letting the Romans off the hook would find their heads between their legs. *Any one,* and that included those of his own blood, for he had more than enough time to sire and raise new sons that would not disappoint him!

Arnak had stood silent during his beating. He showed no sign that he even felt the blows of his father. He stood still until Attila finally dropped back to his couch, exhausted and drunk, to mumble about his new sons. He would sire new sons. Arnak turned his back on his father, but before he did, he took note of the faces there and which ones showed any sign of pleasure at his humiliation.

The next week, Attila announced that he would take a new bride, one young enough to bear him new sons.

Ch'ing Li was there. He saw the steel in Arnak's eye when Attila said he would sire new sons. And now Attila was taking a bride, some slut named Ildico, another cow for his herd. She was the daughter of some obscure chieftain of a nondescript tribe who wished an alliance with the house of Attila. A goat herder could have an alliance with Attila if he had a pretty enough daughter.

He knew that Arnak was the one, for if his father disowned him, he would have nothing, and the lust for the throne of the Hun nation was one he had been brought up with. It was always known that he was the one who would inherit the power upon his father's death. Now that was threatened.

Ch'ing Li sought him out. In the quiet of Arnak's tent, he spoke of the tragedy that was about to befall the prince. It was such an unfair thing to have happen to one that had always been loyal. When Ch'ing Li left Arnak, it was with an unspoken understanding that if Ch'ing could help him in this matter, so that the succession of Arnak would be secure, the prince would be grateful, very grateful.

Ch'ing Li had been careful not to make any mention of what he had in mind, but there had been no need. Both of them understood what was meant by the disguised innuendos used in their conversation.

Ildico was brought to Attila in a caravan escorted by his own guard; and without further delay, they were married according to the rites of the steppes. She knelt before her master under the stars and swore to him that she was untouched and pure. She licked salt from his palm, then placed his right foot on top of her head to signify his mastery over her and her unquestioning obedience to his will.

Ch'ing Li even thought the girl had some merits. She was a very beautiful woman. One who would not be out of place in the collection of a King of Chin. Her eyes were almond-shaped pools of deep brown. She wore the wealth of her tribe on her person. Coins of gold hung in ripples from her neck. In a band on her forehead were precious stones and gems. A belt of gold set with amber was cinched in over her hips—wide, ripe hips that, as Attila had said, were fit for the bearing of sons.

During the feast that followed the ceremony, Ch'ing Li mingled with the guests, making polite conversation about the beauty of his master's new bride, wishing Attila long life and health. The party soon deteriorated into one of their normal drunken brawls with the noble leaders of the Huns vomiting on themselves or dragging slave girls to their couches to copulate with to the cheers of their compatriots.

Ch'ing Li observed them all with contempt and wondered how he had ever thought they were worth his efforts. But he had spent too many years with them now to throw all his work away. He made his way to Attila lying on his couch playing with Ildico's breasts. There he bowed low, kneeling before his master to offer him a gift from Chin. Attila was pleased when he unwrapped the small package. Inside was a ring of massive gold with a carved emerald the size of a thumbnail bearing the relief of a dragon cut with exquisite detail.

Ch'ing Li told Attila, "Here, my Lord and Master, is a gift of luck, for the dragon is the emblem of good fortune and fertility. It would be an honor if you would wear my gift on this your wedding night that the power of the dragon may aid you in siring a new son."

Attila put the ring on his finger, admiring the stone in its raised setting. He smiled at Ch'ing Li. "Thank you, scholar. This is a fine gift. I am pleased to see that you still have my interests at heart. I will wear your gift as a sign of my favor."

Ch'ing had accomplished his mission. He bowed his way out of Attila's presence, pleased and contented that his task had been accomplished so easily.

Arnak cornered him by the fires on which were roasting a full-grown oxen. "When will you do the deed?"

Ch'ing Li smiled smugly. "It is already done, young Lord. It is already done. . . ."

Attila left the crowd for his bed, dragging Ildico behind him. His chieftains and guests cried out for him to prove the mastery of his race, for her and him to ride well and long this night.

In his tent, Attila stripped as Ildico lay nude before him on his couch covered with cloths of gold and silk. Attila admired the beauty of his new bride, the firmness of her breasts and the warm feel of her flesh. Looking down at her, he touched the dragon ring with his other hand, smoothing it over the stone. As his finger ran over the carving, he thought of the night before him. Even with his head swimming in alcohol fumes, he knew that he had a prize to take.

The stone on its raised setting turned under his fingers as he played with it. He felt a sting on his finger and cursed. The ring obviously had a spot that needed to be buffed down. But right now he had more important things on his mind to consider than a scratch.

He lowered himself onto the waiting body of Ildico . . .

Ch'ing was in his tent when he heard the scream. He

smiled and rolled over to go back to sleep. The ring had done its work. Ch'ing knew that in time Attila would play with the setting, and when he did, death would strike and he would be far from the scene of the crime.

It was Harmatta and Arnak who first entered the tent and found Attila lying on his back, mouth filled with blood. Harmatta quickly examined the corpse for any sign of a wound. There was none. Arnak looked down at the body of his father; gone was the power that had struck fear into all that met him. Now he was nothing but a piece of dead meat awaiting the worms.

"Well," he demanded. "What killed him? Was it the slut?" He pointed at a terrified Ildico covering her naked body with a blue silk coverlet.

Harmatta smelled the blood at Attila's gaping mouth; there was no odor. "No, she did nothing. His heart has burst." Harmatta had seen more than one death like this where an older man had died while in the saddle mounting a young filly.

Arnak said nothing, though he knew that it was more than coincidence his father had died this night. He grabbed Ildico by the hair. Twisting her face back, he hissed at her, "Did he spill his seed into you?"

She shook her head no. He had just thrown his head back, clutched his chest and fallen on her dead in the middle of the mating act.

Arnak whispered in her ear. "That had better be true, slut. For now I am the master here. You will leave this place at first light and return to the pigsty from which you came. If you are not gone by then, I will bury you with my father to serve him in the afterlife." Arnak had already thought of the reward he would give to Ch'ing Li for this service. He grinned at the idea.

For three days there was a period of mourning for Attila. His warriors slashed deep cuts in their faces and chests that the master should be mourned, not only with the wailing of women, but also with the blood of warriors. This mourning for his father was to be the greatest in the living memory of man.

The body of Attila was placed in the center of a nearby plain in his silk tent for all to see. Around him were put the spoils of his wars. Gold and silver in amounts too great to count. Bolts of precious silk and cloths of gold. The wealth of nations filled the tent. His body had been prepared by Harmatta who had cleansed his master, then oiled the remains with a mixture of precious herbs and rare spices. In his hand on his chest, Attila held his sword. Around the tent in a circle, twenty thousand warriors rode for two days until they dropped from exhaustion.

The shamans of the tribes gathered in groups to make sacrifices so that the spirits of the elements would protect their master and welcome him as another god. Animals by the hundreds were sacrificed. Their blood gathered and spilled on the dirt around his funeral tent.

Once the mourning was over, his personal bodyguard, under the watchful eye of Arnak and a few of Attila's closest friends and advisors, escorted the remains away from the plain to a small valley, a day's ride away, where a crypt had been prepared to receive him. It was built of massive stones and contained all the wealth of Attila. His sarcophagus was threefold in construction. First a coffin of iron, then one of silver, and the last, in which the Master of the Huns would sleep, was made of gold.

A dozen female slaves were ritually raped by the warriors of the escort, each woman taking at least ten men into her. They spilled their seed into the slaves' bodies, then strangled them with silken cords and set them around the corpse. In the afterlife they would bring forth out of their spirits, by benefit of the seeds placed in them, warriors to serve him. His favorite horses were likewise killed and placed in the tomb along with all the trappings and harnesses, saddles and the articles of war which he would need.

Ch'ing Li stood by Arnak observing the barbaric funeral practices. Arnak stood on top of the tomb and cried out to the men of his father's tribes gathered there: "Lords and nobles, warriors and priests. In my father's tomb are those things he will need to serve him in the afterlife as a great king. He has his women, his weapons, horses and gold. There are the seeds of warriors waiting to be born in the bodies of his women. But he needs one thing more." The audience was silent. Arnak grinned at Ch'ing. "He will need the one whose advice he always valued more than anyone else's. He needs the sage from the land of Chin to go with him and serve him for eternity."

Ch'ing Li felt his heart drop. Arnak pointed to him with a sword crying out to the guards: "Let it be done."

Willing hands grabbed him, jerking him to his knees. His protests were cut off when his breath was stopped by the silk cord around his neck. For a moment he felt the blood pounding in his temples. He tried to cry out, but the swelling heaviness in his head drove everything out of him. Spots whirled before his eyes, then the dark redness telescoped in and he died.

Arnak smiled in a manner resembling that of the now-deceased sire as Ch'ing struggled under the twisting cord. *How could I have ever trusted you, little man? What you would do to my father, you would also have done to me. As Attila always said, do the deed first.*

Arnak had Ch'ing Li's body placed at the foot of his father, along with his everpresent set of scrolls. Then he had the slaves, who had dug the pit for the tomb—three hundred of them—killed by the guards, and they were placed around the outside of the crypt.

The guard and nobles that had gathered filled in the grave. The nobles and escort rode away, leaving only Arnak with his personal troops behind. Once they had left, he took his men and rode to the end of the valley four miles to the north.

There on the banks of the river he gave his final orders concerning the burial of his father. Since the day of his father's death, slaves had been hacking away at the banks of the river until only a wall of earth separated it from the entrance to the valley. Once that barrier was removed the river would follow a new course. The grave of Attila would be forever lost to the eyes of man.

Arnak gave the order and the slaves opened the way letting the waters of the river rush into the valley, flooding it as it south its new course. Once this was done he had his archers kill the slaves.

When he returned to his camp, the archers of his escort were put to death by those that had remained behind. Arnak took no chances. Now he was the only one who knew the exact location of the crypt. The treasure that had been buried with Attila would be there if he ever needed it.

From a distant hill, a lone rider watched the proceedings that ended in the burial of the master of the Huns. The manner in which his fur robes were embroidered, with runic symbols of luck, said that he was from the tribes of the northern Vandals and an ally of the Hun. A closer look would show blue-gray eyes set in a scarred face. Casca had been ordered to go into the territory of the Huns and the Gepids. He was one of the few Romans who knew enough of the tongue of the tribes and their customs to be able to pass for a barbarian warrior if he was questioned.

As the waters of the diverted river erased all evidence of the burial site of Attila, he marked the spot in his mind taking a sight on several landmarks that time would not soon eliminate. It occurred to him as he watched, as it did to Arnak, that there might come a time when knowing where Attila and his treasure was buried—could come in handy.

He turned his horse away. There would be no need to return to Italy. The Huns would not come again, at least not for some time. With the death of Attila there was no one left to hold the thousand tribes together. Casca knew from long experience that soon there would be civil war among the tribes of the Huns as their leaders fought for supreme power. Then, once the division between their masters was evident, the vassal tribes would be quick to try and reassert themselves and regain their own independence. The Huns might come again but not until they found another Attila.

A warm evening breeze rode with him. In three day's time he would be able to see the clean, high, snow-covered peaks of the Alps. The past months had wearied him. He was even afraid to love. Perhaps in the clean air of the Alps where few men went, he would be able to find peace again for a time. At least he wouldn't have to think; and time meant nothing.

Hunched over in his saddle, he let his body sway with the easy gait of the horse, lulling him with the motion. The last thought he had before closing his eyes to sleep was how good it would be to have centuries just slip away from him while he slept the long sleep of eternity.